About the Author

As a nurse by trade, but writer by heart, Paige is a new author from Detroit, Michigan who brings a fresh voice to the already thriving fiction category of romance. Bringing in her own twists and turns full of suspense and "edge-of-your-seat" reading, Paige will pull you right into the pages and bring this tale as old as time to life.

Escape

Paige Spencer

Escape

Vanguard Press

VANGUARD PAPERBACK

© Copyright 2023
Paige Spencer

A CIP catalogue record for this title is
available from the British Library.

ISBN 978 1 80016 966 1

*Vanguard Press is an imprint of
Pegasus Elliot Mackenzie Publishers Ltd.*
www.pegasuspublishers.com

First Published in 2023

**Vanguard Press
Sheraton House Castle Park
Cambridge England**

Printed & Bound in Great Britain

Chapter One

The sound of shattered glass rang throughout the apartment. He hadn't been home for hours. I called him, over and over again, and all I heard was ringing followed by voicemail after voicemail until eventually, I wasn't even granted the courtesy of ringing. Straight to voicemail. He said he was leaving to get food from the restaurant up the street, and it's been over four hours. I'm not even sure why I'm calling. Must be habit. Because if I'm being honest, I wish he'd stay gone. But just as I begin to pray that he won't come back, I hear the door swing open. And I am already missing the sound of his voicemail. While it gave me no insight to where he was, or if he was safe, at least it was the voice of a kinder man. The man I often pretended he still was. But tonight, he was not that man. Tonight, he's the angry, brutal person whose voice came booming through the thick air. Air so thick I could barely breathe, barely think. My adrenaline spiked and my ears started to ring. My heart rate began to elevate, and my palms began to sweat. All I could do was sit in the bed, in the darkness, waiting for the storm to roll in, waiting for him.

I feel like I was woken up with a jolt of electricity; it felt like two paddles were slammed to my chest in an attempt to revive me. I was doused in a cold sweat. The kind where your fingers are ice-cold and goosebumps cover your body, but your core feels like an inferno. My palms are soaking, my hair is matted to my forehead, and my heart racing. The nightmares. Again. They have come and gone since I arrived here. Except unlike normal nightmares, like teeth falling out or reading an English assignment naked in front of your peers, I can't convince myself that this 'wasn't real'. Because it was real. And I lived it on repeat every day for five years. Held captive by his kind words and empty apologies.

I grab my phone and wince at the bright artificial light that illuminates my room: 3.35 a.m. I need sleep. I think about the job interview I have in the morning and I need to be well rested. I lie back down, stare at the ceiling and try to focus on the humming of the fan, a much-needed white noise that I can only hope will lull me back to sleep. I toss and turn, unable to find comfort. After what feels like hours, I realize my hopes of peace will go unanswered. I check my phone again: 5.15 a.m. Finally giving up on any chance of sleep, I get out of bed and head to the bathroom.

I splash my face with cold water, too cold. It takes forever for the water to get warm in this little apartment. I brush my teeth and pull my unruly hair into a bun and throw on my nearest sports bra and leggings. The sun is just starting to peek through the windows and the room glows a beautiful golden color. I grab my headphones, pop them in and tuck my phone into the pocket on my leggings.

I step out on the small porch that leads me down two stairs and my feet hit the pavement. I've never been much of a runner. I never actually understood why runners enjoyed running. The burn in your chest, gasping for air; it never appealed to me. That was until I had something to run from. The nightmares, the screaming, the tears… they all seem to get quieter with each slam to the pavement. To be honest, I'm not the best runner. I walk a lot in between and probably look like I'm an inch from death, but I would do anything to keep the peace it provides.

My watch chimes, ONE MILE as I come up to my favorite coffee shop. I haven't been here long, but this coffee shop has already become a little oasis for me. I'm here almost every day and order the same thing every time. After giving myself a chance to catch my breath I walk up to the counter.

"Caramel latte with almond milk please. Oh, and a blueberry scone." I don't even know why I bother saying my order as the sandy-haired barista laughs.

"So, the usual? Are you ever gonna mix it up?" he says in a thick English accent. "For here too?" he says with a friendly laugh he turns as he starts my order.

"Creature of habit, I guess. And yes please." I offer a smile before leaving to find the table right by the window. The sun is almost up now, shining on the cobblestone streets that look like they were plucked right from a classic novel. Most of the buildings in this town are red brick with old wooden windows. It feels romantic, and safe. The barista pulls me from my thoughts and sets my order on the table.

"Thank you so much." I offer another smile as I grab my drink and take a sip. That first sip of hot coffee is my favorite. It brings a warmth throughout my body and a calmness into my mind. All of my muscles and worries seem to relax more and more with each sip. Once I finish, I put my headphones back in and walk a couple streets over to the farmer's market. This is my favorite market around here. They had them back home, but not like this. I walk from stand to stand and grab just enough groceries to make dinner this evening. My apartment has a very small fridge, so I typically buy just enough groceries to get me through the day. I buy my last item, a head of lettuce, from a young brown haired-boy who can't be older than fourteen, then I head back towards the apartment.

The place is small, but for me it's just perfect. The wall to the left as you walk in is exposed brick that looks like it has been there since the beginning of time. Straight ahead are skinny stairs that lead upstairs to the only bedroom and bathroom. The stairs are old and creak with every step. To the right is the small living room, just big enough for a two-seater couch and a small coffee table. I haven't had the chance to bother with a TV just yet, and probably won't. Then in the back of the small apartment is the kitchen. The fridge is just as tall as me and the stove requires a match to turn it on. The apartment has a draft, the plumbing leaks, and you can hear every neighbor around you through the paper-thin walls. But it's mine. And it's perfect.

I head up the noisy stairs and straight to the bathroom. I have an interview today at a local diner. I've never been in the service industry before, but I need a job and quick. I head in the shower and let the warmth take over my aching muscles. As usual, I only have about fifteen minutes of warm water before it turns ice-cold, so I'm out fast. I step out, wrapping a towel over myself and my hair. I walk up to the mirror, wipe off the fog, and give myself a mini pep-talk. I'm nervous. I've never been to a foreign country, let alone tried to get a job in one. I chose England because my younger self was always interested in what it could offer. I loved it before I had ever been there and would daydream about moving here. And as soon as I arrived, I felt it. I felt the peace this place offered me. I ended up in Hampstead with a population less than 7,000. I liked that it was small, friendly, and relatively unknown. I frequented a small diner up the street and one day decided to ask the owner about a job. It's walking distance to my apartment and everyone there seems really friendly.

I dry my hair, throw a few curls in it and put just enough make-up on to hide my lack of sleep. I walk over to my closet that's about the size of a small coat closet, but I don't mind it. I don't have much anyways. I grab a white button-down shirt and a pair of black pants. I slip into my most comfortable heels and give myself a once-over in the full-length mirror that's on the inside of the closet door. I smooth my clothes and try to rid them of any wrinkles. I've had many job interviews in the past, but I really need this one. I probably need this one more than any other job I've applied to in the past. I didn't come here with a lot of money, and what I did bring is running low already. Not to mention, I'll need a work visa to stay more permanently, as long as everything goes to plan. I've only been here for two weeks, but Hampstead is not a cheap place to live and it's wringing me dry.

I walk down the stairs, grab my bag, and head out the door. It's only eight a.m., and my interview isn't until nine, but I like to walk slow and take in the city around me. The beautiful streets, each little shop with its own personality, people enjoying breakfast on small patios that line the streets. It's beautiful. It looks just how I imagined it would when I was a teenager eager to travel the world. I felt so free at that age, like I could do anything in the world. While I'm only thirty now, I feel like I've aged twice that. After a thirty-minute walk, which could have easily been fifteen minutes, I arrive at the diner. I walk up to the young hostess.

"Excuse me, my name is Payton. I have an interview at nine a.m."

I offer my warmest smile and try not to look nervous or out of place. She looks up at me wide-eyed, probably surprised by my American accent.

"Uh, yeah. Sure, one moment." She walks to the back of the diner and disappears behind two swinging doors. After a few minutes she returns with an older woman. The woman looks very kind with a smile on her face. She reaches her hand out to me.

"Payton? Good morning! My name is Laura," she says in a thick accent as she shakes my hand. "Early to the interview? Good sign," she adds with a wink and a warm smile. She directs me over to a table in the back of the restaurant and I follow. The diner is small but full of little round tables. The ceiling is tall with wooden beams lining it and the walls are exposed brick. There is a small wood-burning fireplace against one of the walls that make the entire room smell amazing. The place feels very welcoming and warm.

The interview lasts longer than I expected, but we were caught up in laughs and commonalities. Laura is a very sweet woman with a daughter my age and a granddaughter she adores. She has a very warm personality that makes you feel like you've known her for a lifetime. She offered me the job at the end of the interview and eagerly asks when I can start.

"Um, as soon as possible I guess," I say with a laugh.

"How about we bring you in tomorrow? It's a Thursday which is usually a slower day, so it'll give you some practice before the busy weekend."

We stand together and I agree. I want nothing more than this place to feel like home, and a job is definitely a good start.

Chapter Two

It's about ten thirty when I leave the interview. I kill an hour or two by strolling around the other shops around the diner. There are some other bars, another diner, some clothing stores, and a bookstore. I go into each shop, purposely leaving the bookstore for last. I've always enjoyed reading occasionally, but since arriving here it's the only hobby I have. I don't know anyone here and I've never been the most extroverted person. So, I spend my time reading, which I honestly prefer.

I walk into the bookstore and it has that wonderful 'old bookstore' smell. It's intoxicating. The place seems small at first, but I soon realize it's long and skinny with books from floor to ceiling. It looks like it has books for miles. Old books, new books, books in other languages. I walk through the entire place reading almost every book title I see, passing a ladder on each wall that extends all the up the ten-foot ceilings. As I make my way back to the front of the store, a dark-haired man walks up to the counter. His hair lies over his forehead with a part down the middle, like a 1990s Leonardo DiCaprio. It's so dark, almost black. My eyes scan his arms that are full of tattoos; his nails are painted black, and his fingers are covered in silver rings. His black short-sleeved button-up shirt has just enough buttons undone to see that his arms aren't the only areas covered in tattoos.

"Can I help you?" he says as he looks at me through the hair that lies over his eyebrows. He smiles at me with a wide smile showing perfect teeth. His accent isn't quite as thick as others I've heard; he's much easier to understand. His exterior is tough, but he radiates warmth.

"Um, yeah, I guess. Any recommendations? Something that people here find popular?" I ask.

He furrows his brow. "Hm, I'm not really up on what's popular, unless you're into sparkling vampires which seem to be all the rage. But if you're looking to take a bit of a risk…" He eyes a small basket in front of the counter. It's full of books wrapped in brown parchment so you can't see the cover. On the front of each book is a handwritten description of the plot. The sign on the front on the basket says, 'Don't Judge a Book by the Cover' . I grab one right on top and the description is about a girl starting her first year at college where she meets a boy opposite her, and they fall in love. Very clichéd, but I live for cheesy love stories.

"I guess we'll go with this one," I say and offer a small smile and place the book on the small glass counter. I grab my wallet and the dark-haired man holds up his hand.

"It's on the house," he smiles. He must notice the confused look on my face because he continues. "I mean, just bring it back when you're done, and you can switch it out with another one from the basket."

"Oh, are you sure?" I ask timidly.

He runs his hand through his thick hair and smiles, "I haven't seen you in here before. Are you new to the area?" he asks ignoring my question.

"Erm, yeah I am. That obvious, huh?" I chuckle knowing that it is very obvious that I am not from around here.

"A bit," he laughs. "Well, I hope you enjoy the book, and I hope to see you next time." He offers a kind smile, and he watches me leave the store as I thank him again.

I walk down the road a bit more. It's now past lunch time and all I had for breakfast was my usual scone, so I step inside a small restaurant and order lunch to-go. I'm eager to get back and read my new find.

I step into my apartment and walk to the kitchen. After putting my groceries away, I place my lunch onto a plate and pour myself an iced tea. I take it to the small couch and place my plate on the coffee table. I rummage through my bag, find the book, and begin to read.

What feels like an hour ends up being four when I realize I've read to the middle of the book. The book wasn't necessarily a long one, but I didn't expect to be so drawn in so much. I only picked at my lunch because I couldn't pull myself away from the story, so I pack it up into a Tupperware container and put it in the fridge, then remembering my groceries from earlier. I've always preferred take-out over cooking. At least I won't have to buy a lunch tomorrow for work, or dinner.

I grab a bottle of wine from the counter and pour myself a glass. I walk over to the living room window and watch people stroll by. I love people watching, especially in a place so new to me. I love hearing their accents as their conversations pass my window. Mothers pushing their infants in strollers, couples walking hand in hand, groups of friends walking to the nearest pub. I still feel like a stranger here, like I'm just visiting. It hasn't quite hit me that this is supposed to home now, and I have no plans to leave, hopefully.

I finish off my first glass of wine and pour myself another as I sit back on the couch. The sun is starting to set and offers a warm glow into the apartment. I turn on the lamp next to the couch and continue to read, immersing myself back into the mind of a young college girl with the world at her feet, falling in love with a boy her mother doesn't approve of, but finding her happily ever after against all odds. Before I know it, it's half past midnight and I've finished the book. Once I put the book down, I realize just how tired I am. I put the wine glass in the sink and head upstairs to bed. A little fuzzy from the wine, my brain drifts off to sleep with images of black nail polish and serving trays.

Chapter Three

Having slept better than the night before, I woke up right at five a.m. feeling rested. I head to the bathroom to get ready for my morning run. My first shift at the diner is today, but not until eight a.m. I have some 'first day' nerves and I'm hoping a good run with shake them. I usually hate 'first anythings', but especially first days of work. I always feel like everyone's eyes are on me and I'm not one to enjoy any attention. But of course, it's unavoidable. So, I tell myself to just muster through it until I'm regular enough to blend in with everyone else. That's all I want: to blend in.

I put my headphones in my ears and my playlist full of high-tempo songs fills my ears. My run took its usual route, stopping at my favorite coffee shop to start off the rest of my morning. I walk up to the counter and the barista from yesterday, and almost every day before that, is there. It must be his regular shift. He looks up at me and raises his eyebrow with a smile.

"The usual?" He smiles.

I casually look at the menu as if I'm not going to order that same thing. Faking my best 'thinking' face.

After a moment I look at him and laugh.

"Yeah, you already know. Who am I kidding?" I cave. I walk over to my usual table. I look around the coffee shop and find that I'm the only one here this morning. It's so peaceful as the sunrise fills the coffee shop and I look out at those beautiful cobblestone streets I admire every day. The barista walks up and places my order in front of me. I thank him and begin to drink my coffee.

"You Americans and your coffee," he says with a teasing tone and a kind smile.

"You Brits and your tea," I reply with a laugh and take another sip.

He laughs, "Okay, fair enough." He goes to turn away but turns back towards me.

"My name is Noah, by the way."

"Um, Payton," I reply, and I look up at him.

"Nice to meet you, Payton." He smiles. He smiles a lot.

"So, my girlfriend and I just moved here from the city a few months ago and we don't really know anyone," he continues.

"Oh?" I reply.

"And I thought maybe you'd like to hit the pub with us one of these nights. Ya know, just a couple of newbies." His offer is very kind.

"Is it that obvious that I'm new around here?" I laugh. Clearly, I don't blend in here as much as I thought. I must have *newbie* or *lost* tattooed on my forehead.

"Only a little." Noah laughs. I pounder his offer for just a moment. It would be nice to have a friend, or two, here. As much as I love to sit at home, it has been feeling a little more lonely than usual.

"Sure, I'd love to actually, it'd be nice to make some friends here." I accept his offer and we agree to meet up this weekend where I can meet his girlfriend, Olivia. After we exchange phone numbers, I finish up my scone, wave goodbye to Noah, and walk back to the apartment.

I begin to get ready for my first day at the diner. I feel nervous but excited to be placing some roots here. I jump out of the shower that turned cold much sooner than usual. I dry my hair and tie it back into a slick ponytail. I dress in the black shirt and khakis that Laura stated as dress code in the interview. I will have to go buy more pants after my shift today, this is my only pair of khakis and I do not want to be at the laundromat every night. I grab my bag and toss in my lunch from yesterday and the book from the bookstore. I'll stop there after my shift.

I get to the diner and Laura comes up to me immediately and pulls me into a hug.

"Happy first day! I'll show you where to put your stuff. You'll shadow Lily today," she says as she introduces me to Lily, a petite brown-haired girl with a kind smile and soft voice.

The morning was slow, as predicted by Laura, which gave me the opportunity to ask Lily a lot of questions. Lily is very kind and answers every single one. If my questions were annoying, she hid it well. The lunch rush was a little more hectic, but I was already getting the hang of things by then. Lily even let me take a few tables by myself before the end of the shift. As my shift came to a close, I grabbed my stuff out of my locker in the break room. I thank Lily for her patience with me and I say goodbye to some of the other coworkers I met on my shift today. Everyone was very friendly, including the patrons, and I feel like I'm going to really like working here.

I walk down the street to the clothing store I stopped in yesterday and grabbed a couple pairs of khakis and a few black collared shirts. I check out with a soft-spoken girl that raised her eyebrow at my accent. Another reminder that I am not from around here. I walk out of the store and almost forgot about swapping my book at the bookstore before I saw the old wooden sign swinging outside the door. Barett's Books was carved into the sign.

I walk into the bookstore and up to the counter. No one is at the counter, so while I wait, I look through the basket full of the 'mystery' books. After a few minutes someone walks out from the back and up to the counter. I look up and found myself oddly disappointed when I see a dark-hair girl.

"Can I help you?" she asks; her voice is very kind.

"Um, I got this book yesterday and the guy here before told me I could bring it back and swap it out for another one," I say, feeling awkward and wondering if he was supposed to let me do that.

"Oh of course! Feel free!" she says as she holds her hand out towards the basket. Feeling relieved, I drop the old book back into the basket and nod to her with the new book in hand. I get to the door to leave as a hear a familiar voice behind me.

"There's no way you finished that book already!"

It's the guy from yesterday. He's walking towards me dressed in a leather jacket, black jeans with holes in the knees, and a pair of worn-out black boots. His neck is filled with silver necklaces and I must not have noticed the silver hoop in his nose yesterday. I can't help but admit to myself that he's attractive, like really attractive.

"Um, actually yes." I laugh. "It was really good, and I honestly don't have much of a social life." I clench my jaw as I can't believe I just admitted to this stranger that I lack a social life.

He laughs as he runs his hand through his hair. His laugh is much warmer than his appearance.

"What's next on the reading list?" he asks as he looks at the book in my hands.

I look down at the description of the book written on the cover and read: "'Tender story about the enduring power of love. Set amid the austere beauty of coastal North Carolina in 1946'."

"Hopeless romantic, huh?" he asks, but not in a judgmental *I can't believe this chick reads this crap* way.

"I guess you could say that," I reply as I offer him a warm, slightly awkward, smile. He looks up at me through his shaggy hair, his eyes almost as dark as his hair.

"Well, I hope you enjoy it," he replies and offers me another kind smile. I nod and walk out of the bookstore. I get about ten steps down and hear the bell of the bookstore's door ding behind me, signaling someone else has walked out. I turn around and see the man outside, lighting a cigarette and holding it between his black painted fingers. I watch him take a deep inhale that turns into a large puff of smoke around him. He ashes the cigarette and takes another hit and his other hand runs through his hair. Just as I realize I'm staring, he does too, and he smiles. As his eyes meet mine, I turn around quickly and head back down the road, my face beet red I'm sure.

Chapter Four

The next two days at work flew by. Laura was right, the weekends get very busy. By the time my shift was done on Saturday, I was exhausted. Just as I started to daydream about getting into my pajamas and continuing to read the book I got from the bookstore a few days ago, I remember the plans I made with Noah, the barista. I told him I'd meet his girlfriend and him at a local pub this evening. I was trying to come up with an excuse to tell Noah so I could bail, but the best I come up with is food poisoning, which is the world's most used *I'm trying to get out of something* lie. So, I suck it up and text Noah to confirm the time.

ME: Hey! What time should I meet you guys?

NOAH: We were thinking eight p.m.! Is that okay?

ME: Sure! See you there ☺

That's an hour and a half from now. That gives me just enough time to shower the smell of diner food off me and look semi-decent.

I head back to the apartment. As much as I'd like to stay in and read, I'm also looking forward to making some new friends here. I can't spend my life here locked up in my apartment; even a homebody like me will get stir crazy eventually. I change from my greasy diner uniform and step into my favorite pair of black jeans and a grey sweater. I dry my hair that's still soaking wet from the shower and put some loose curls into it. I decide to pull half of it back and let my blonde bangs frame my face. I dust on some black mascara and some blush to help me look more awake. I put on my only pair of black combat boots, that have definitely seen better days, and head out.

The pub isn't very far from the apartment, so I pass on a taxi and decide to walk. I get to the pub and see Noah and a strikingly beautiful woman next to him, that must be his girlfriend, Olivia. Noah is also very handsome, so it makes sense that his girlfriend is just as striking. Once Noah gets eyes on me, he starts waving at me to signal me over. I walk up to the high-top table they're seated at.

Noah begins introductions.

"Olivia, this is Payton. She's a regular at the café. Payton, this is my girlfriend, Olivia." I hold out my hand to shake Olivia's and she grabs it and pulls me into hug that I was not expecting.

"It's so nice to meet you! Noah was telling me you're also new to the area." Her accent is beautiful, easy to understand, and she seems so kind. Olivia has perfectly curled shiny brown hair that goes to the middle of her back. Her smile shows beautifully white teeth and a perfectly angled jaw. She's so pretty it's intimidating, even though she is actually the opposite of intimidating.

"Um yeah, I'm definitely far from home," I say and my stomach knots. "Well, this is home now, but you know what I mean." I laugh off the feeling in my gut. Noah,

Olivia, and I go on to order a few drinks and asks questions like we're all on a first date.

"So, what brings you to Hampstead?" Noah asks.

"I guess I was just looking for a change," I say keeping it light, and short. "You guys?"

"Olivia's job transferred her here," Noah explains.

"Oh?" I say as I look at Olivia. "What do you do?" I ask.

"I'm in publishing, and they opened a new office out here, so I came to help get it going." She smiles.

Small banter like this continues. I learned that Noah was a teacher but couldn't find any jobs near here when they moved, so he's working at the coffee shop until he finds a teaching position. He worked at a coffee shop as a teen, so it was familiar to him and easy to pick up again. They've been together for three years and have lived in England their entire lives. They are the perfect couple. Although, as I know first-hand, looks can be deceiving. But overall, they do seem very happy.

I'm a few drinks in and starting to feel a little less nervous than I did at the beginning. Olivia is telling me a story about how they adopted their cat, Snowball, when I see a familiar face walk into the pub.

It's the guy, from the bookstore. He's wearing the same leather jacket I saw him in earlier. He's wearing a thick chunky necklace with a small lock on it and his usual row of rings on his fingers. What I didn't notice before was the tattoos that also ran across his knuckles. He has a cigarette tucked behind one of his ears and has a small cross earring hanging from the other. He's here with a couple friends dressed in the same dark aesthetic, but he definitely sticks out more than the others.

Olivia must have noticed me observing him as she interrupts my thoughts, "Do you know him?" she asks.

"Um, not really. He works at the bookstore I go to," I explain.

"Oh, so you don't hang out with him?" Her question seems weird.

"Oh, no. Why?" I ask.

"I mean, I've just overheard things, ya know?" She shrugs.

"Like?" My curiosity is piqued.

"Just that he doesn't run with the most proper crowd. He seems nice and all though." Olivia looks at him quickly and turns away with flushed cheeks when he notices her staring. Even she's intimidated by him. His eyes scan from her to me. When he sees me at the table, he gives me a large smile. I looked down, a little embarrassed and notice my drink is empty. I excuse myself from the table to go to the bar to order another.

I get to the bar and order another glass of wine. As I wait, I feel someone walk up and stand next to me.

"Hey! Good to see you having a social life," the dark-haired man says with a wink and a smile.

"Oh hey!" I look up at him. "Yeah, I figured it was time to put the books down. It isn't going anywhere, I guess." My cheeks flush at my bad joke, if you could even call it that.

"What's your name, by the way? I figured if I'd be seeing you at the bookstore more often, I should know your name," he asks. His eyes are kind yet piercing.

"Um, Payton." I clear my throat. "And yours?" I ask as my wine arrived from the bartender.

"Samuel, or Sam," he states as he holds his hand out. "Nice to meet you."

I place my hand in his and he gently squeezes down. His rings are cold against my palm.

"Are you uh… here with someone?" He glances around the bar.

"Just a couple of friends," I say as I point to Olivia and Noah who are cuddled together, looking like I'm a third wheel on their date.

"Oh, very cool," he says. I go to pay for my wine and he gently grabs my hand. "Ben, put hers on my tab," he tells the bartender. My eyes go wide.

"Oh, you don't have to do that, really…" I feel embarrassed.

"I know." He looks at me with a soft smile, runs his hand through his hair, his signature I'm noticing, and walks away back to his table of friends.

I go back to the table with Noah and Olivia, finish my wine, and tell them that I am going to head home. Olivia gives me a big hug and tells me how nice it was to meet me, and I tell her the same. Noah pulls me in for a hug as well and insists we hang out again. I assure him that we will.

I walk out of the bar and start towards the direction of my apartment. As I'm walking, I hear the thud of heavy boots come up behind me. I turn around and see Samuel jogging towards me.

"Leaving so soon?" he asks.

"Um, yeah. Work was pretty exhausting today, so I'm heading home," I explain.

"Um, alone?" he says, his eyes wide.

"Yes," I reply, feeling like that's the wrong answer.

"Um, I know you're new here, but you shouldn't be walking around the city this late at night... alone."

He shifts uncomfortably, his tone trying not to offend me.

"Well, I mean I don't have a car. And I feel like taking the taxis are almost worse than walking alone." I laugh softly.

"Well, I mean my friends are gonna be at the pub awhile, I wouldn't mind walking you back." He runs his hands through his hair. "If that's okay?" he asks.

"Um, sure. I guess." I shrug. We start walking towards my apartment, although my pace has slowed drastically with the addition of Samuel.

"So, what brought you to Hampstead? You're obviously from the States." God, I hate that question.

"Um, just needed a change of scenery," I reply, giving as little as possible.

Samuel laughs, "You're telling me all of America looks the exact same? That's a far trip just to change some scenery." He looks as me as we walk.

I laugh. "True. I've just had a thing about wanting to see England since I was a kid. So, I figured it was a good spot to settle."

"Yikes, I'm sure this old town has disappointed you then." He shoves his hands into his pockets.

"Definitely not. This place is beautiful. The cobblestone, the old buildings, the streets filled with shops and farmers markets. This place is perfect. A real-life story book town."

"Speaking of story, what's yours?" He's kind as he asks, genuinely curious.

"Um, still being written, I guess." I feel the twist in my stomach, wishing the subject would change.

"Very cool... mine too, I guess." He looks at me and one side of his mouth curls up into a smile.

We finally get to the door of my apartment.

"Well, this is me. Thank you for walking me back."

"Of course, anytime. I enjoyed it, actually." He smiles big this time. He takes the cigarette out from behind his ear and lights it. He takes a long drag and as he exhales, he blows the smoke away from me.

"It was really nice running into you, Payton." He bows his head, turns around and walks back to the direction of the bar. I watch him as he walks down the road, cigarette smoke surrounding him. He glances back in my direction and sees me watching him, and my cheeks turn red. I'm glad it's dark and he can't see my face flush. I turn around quickly and step into my apartment.

Chapter Five

He stumbles through the bedroom door, and I can already smell the liquor permeating through his entire body. It's almost like he forgets I'm there for just a moment as he stumbles around the room, until he looks up and his eyes meet mine. They're dark, almost black. Void of feeling.

"Don't you fucking judge me," he growls. I don't say anything, I've learned from past mistakes that it's better to stay silent than to speak. I lie in the bed and tighten my eyes.

"Huh?" His voice rises. "You think you're better than me?!" he yells as he stands up straight. I'm frozen. I couldn't speak even if I wanted to.

"You're nothing without me! You understand that?! You don't have shit without me! You leave me, and what will you have? Huh?!" He's getting louder and louder. He pauses a moment and I open my eyes. He's looking around. I watch him spot a glass filled with water that I left on the TV stand. He grabs the glass and hurls it in my direction. I watch the glass get closer to my face, as if it's in slow motion. I hear a bang, and everything goes dark.

I wake up with a gasp, soaked in my own sweat. Another nightmare. My heart is racing, I look around in the dark room around me, reminding me that right now, I'm safe. Everything seems so quiet and so still, in contrast to my nightmare. I grab my phone and squint as I read the time on the bright phone screen: 3.35 a.m. I turn my screen off and lie back on a different pillow as I push my sweaty one to the other side of the bed. When will these stop? Am I cursed to a life of rage-filled dreams? As if I hadn't suffered enough.

After a few restless minutes, I crawl out of bed and head downstairs to get myself a glass of water. As I stand at the sink filling the glass I am reminded of my nightmare. I get a twist in my stomach. I shake my head as the nightmare tries to replay itself. I take a couple sips of water and leave the empty glass in the sink as I head back upstairs. I lie back down on the bed and stare at the ceiling, begging sleep to come.

The next time I open my eyes, it's daylight. I can tell the sleep that finally came was restless by my dry eyes and aching head, but it was sleep, nonetheless. I walk into the bathroom and look at the bags forming under my eyes. I can't tell whether they are from the repeated sleepless nights or the busy shift I worked yesterday. I'm thankful for finding a decent job with nice people but working in food service is no joke.

I jump in the shower and stay until the water goes cold, which took longer than normal, for which I am very appreciative. I step out and begin to dry my hair. I pull it back into a low bun and skip the make up for the day. My bangs hang around my face as I secure my bun with gold hair pins. I pull on my favorite black jeans and a white V-neck T-shirt. It's supposed to be a little warmer today and today is my day off. I head downstairs and start the coffee maker. Due to my exhaustion and a serious need for sleep, I skipped my run this morning. As the coffee brews, I throw some toast in the toaster and pull the blueberry jelly out of the fridge.

I sit down on the couch with my coffee and jellied toast and look outside. The day looks incredible. There's plenty of sunlight, very little wind, and no rain, which isn't typical Hampstead weather this time of year, I think. We are finally in the thick of spring with more warm days than cold ones. I open the book from the bookstore and begin to read it as I finish my coffee. It was a story of an old woman who has dementia, and her husband reads her the story of how they fell in love. Eventually she remembers who he is, and they dance and cry. Until, soon after, she forgets who he is again.

As I finish the last page of the book I am crying into my coffee. I mean, who wouldn't. I gather myself up, grateful that I chose to pass on make up today and put my dishes in the sink. I don't have the luxury of a dishwasher in this small apartment. I throw on a light jean jacket and my pair of dingy black Converses. I grab my bag and head out the door with the book in hand.

I feel nervous as I approach the bookstore. It was just last night when Samuel had walked me home. But he was just being nice, right?

The door chimes as I walk in. I scan the bookstore and see nobody. I place the book down in the pile on parchment covered books and read through a couple different descriptions from the basket. After reading the third science-fiction description in a row, I hear someone come from the back of the store. I look up and see that dark mop of hair walk towards me.

"Payton! How are you?" Samuel asks lightly with a smile ear to ear.

"Um, I'm doing fine. Got back to the bar okay?" I ask.

"Well, I'm alive aren't I?" he laughs and he flaps his arms over his body. His white shirt reads *Ramones* in faded red lettering and his black jeans have holes down their entire length.

I laugh. "Yeah, of course." I look back down to the pile of books and try to shuffle through some other books. I hear that familiar sound of his clunking boots get closer and I look up. Samuel is bringing me a book.

"Here, I think this should be your next read," he says as he stretches his arm out to me.

"*The Great Gatsby*?" I say as I take the book from his hand.

"Have you ever read it? I mean, you probably have," he says, shoving his hands in his pockets. Of course I've read it.

"No," I lie. I'd like to keep things short and sweet today.

"Oh, well, it's my favorite book and I think you'd really like it." I take the book in my hand and scan the cover.

"Oh, thank you." I place the book on the counter and begin to look for my wallet. It didn't come from the basket, so I would like to pay for it.

While running his fingers through his hair he says, "Just bring it back when you're done." He smiles and winks. As he backs up his hair falls over his forehead and covers just the tops of his dark eyes. I smile and thank him again as I turn to leave.

I stop at the grocery store to grab food for tonight and restock on some essentials. I was up too late for the farmer's market. I'm not much of a cook so I keep it simple, noodles with red sauce. I walk through the aisles and grab a few more necessities before paying at the register and walking back to my apartment.

I walk through the door, heavy grocery bags in each hand. I drop the bags on the kitchen counter and wince as I look at the red marks across my fingers. I begin to put the groceries away and look outside. I don't do much on my day off. I don't know anyone here; well, I don't *really* know anyone. My first week here, all I did was walk the neighborhood, over and over again. I did, and still do, find it absolutely amazing here. It's simple yet grand. Old yet new. But the routine gets a bit old.

I walk over to the couch and look at the book. Why does he want me to read his favorite book? He's probably just being nice and is interested in helping a fellow book nerd. I grab it and study the dust jacket. It's very worn, very old. Clearly a popular book or a book that has been sitting in that small bookstore for a long time. I assume the latter. I remove my shoes and curl up on the couch. The sunshine gleaming into the window is the perfect reading light. I toss a blanket over myself, tuck my knees up, and begin to read. I've read the book before, but it's been such a long time. And he *is* right, it's a great book.

Chapter Six

I wake up, book on the floor. I must have dozed off. I check the time: five thirty p.m. Wow, I dozed off for a few hours. I must be more exhausted than I thought. I guess after two weeks of doing close to nothing, starting a new job and meeting new people takes its toll. I walk over to the kitchen and start to boil water for my dinner. Once the water begins to boil, I empty the small box of elbow pasta into the water. I grab the wine off the counter and pour myself a glass.

It doesn't take long for the pasta to cook, and I strain it out and dump the red sauce over the noodles and mix it around. I eat at the counter as I people watch outside of my window.

As I finish dinner along with my second glass of wine, I get a text.

NOAH: Live music at the pub tn, care to join? ☺

I sigh heavily as I contemplate going out again versus staying in. As much as I'm leaning towards staying in, it's all I've done since I arrived here.

ME: I'm in ☺ what time?

NOAH: Eight p.m. See you there!

Eight p.m., that's only an hour and a half from now. I finish up dishes, put my leftover food away, and head upstairs. I decide to keep my low bun but end up putting on some mascara and lip gloss. Olivia will be there and she is so put together, she makes you want to look put together. I add some small gold hooped earrings and thin necklace to match. I walk over to my closet and stare inside. I really don't have much to choose from. When I moved here, I only came with what would fit in a backpack and a small suitcase. I've been slowly adding things since I got here, but there's still little to choose from. I decide to swap out my Converses for my black boots and my jean jacket for a light black jacket.

I leave the apartment with fifteen minutes to spare for the walk there. I hear the echo of Samuel's voice telling me I shouldn't walk alone at night in the city. I hold my bag closer to me and begin to walk faster.

I arrive at the pub and start to scan for Noah and Olivia. I see both of them waving their arms around trying to get my attention. My cheeks flush as I see some of the patrons give them a funny look. I walk over to them and greet them both with a quick hug, leaving one hand in my jacket pocket.

"So, who's supposed to play?" I ask, having to yell over the sound of the full bar.

"Not sure, it's usually the same three bands that rotate different nights," Noah explains.

"Live music means I need a drink." I joke as I step away from the table and walk over to the bar. I've never been a fan of live bar music. Having to yell at those around you just to communicate. Even worse if the band is terrible.

I order a beer off the 'Specials' list and watch the bartender disappear momentarily. He returns from the back with my drink. As I dig my wallet out of my bag to pay the bartender, I hear the full bar start to cheer. I place the money on the bar, grab my drink and turn around. It's hard to get a good look at the band with all these people shuffling in front of the bar. I'm walking back towards the table with Noah and Olivia when I notice the four-person band on the stage in front. The singer has his back to the crowd at first, and when he turns around my eyes widen.

It's Samuel. And he looks straight at me. He smiles ear to ear when he sees me, and I offer a small smile and nervous wave.

He swings a guitar strap over his neck as he looks at me, counts to four out loud, and begins to play while belting out lyrics at the same time, finally breaking eye contact.

I know this song. *This Charming Man*, by The Smiths. Samuel is wearing his leather jacket with a black T-shirt underneath. He's strayed far from his typical black jeans and is wearing red plaid pants with a chain hanging off his hip. He has his signature boots with silver jewelry covering his neck and his fingers. His black hair rests on his forehead as he sings with his eyes closed.

I look at Noah and Olivia and they're singing along with the rest of the bar. With the music making conversation is nearly impossible, I turn my back to them to watch the band as I sip on my drink.

The first song comes to an end and Samuel runs his hands through his hair and waves to the crowd that erupts in applause.

"Thank you! We're Bridges I Burn doing some covers for you tonight. My name is Sam and I hope you have a great time," he says with a wink and a half smile as he goes right into the next song.

Four more songs go by before the band gathers in the center of the stage and takes a bow.

"Thank you! Enjoy the rest of your evening." Samuel says into the mic.

I turn back to Noah and Olivia and listen to Olivia talk about the new intern her job hired today. She likes her, I think.

I notice Olivia's eyes look behind me, then I hear someone holler in my direction.

"Payton!" he yells. I turn around.

"Hey Samuel, um, great set. You were really great," I say with a warm smile. I mean it, it was fantastic.

"Thanks, I didn't know you'd be here," he says as he puts his hands in his pockets.

"I didn't know you were in a band," I reply as a motion my glass towards the empty stage.

He laughs, "Um, I guess. It's just a hobby, something I do to stay out of trouble," he says with a soft smile. "Can I get your next one?" he asks gesturing towards my empty glass.

"Oh, you don't have to do that. Please." I beg. If anything, I owe him for all the books he has let me borrow.

"I know I don't have to, but I'd really like to. I'll be back." He smiles and walks over to the bar before I can protest. I look over at Noah and Olivia who look surprised.

"Um, is he into you or what?" she insinuates loudly.

"I don't think so. He's just a nice guy," I reply.

"Oh, he's totally into you," Noah adds. "He was watching you his whole set." He smiles.

I roll my eyes. "He was not!" I laugh. Samuel is absolutely not into me. We hardly know each other.

"You mentioned yesterday that you didn't know him," Olivia says as she raises her eyebrow with a smile.

"I mean, I've been to the bookstore by my work a few times. He works there," I reply a little more defensively that I mean to. "I thought *you* said he was bad news?" I say jokingly.

"Psh, what do I know?" Olivia laughs back.

Samuel returns with another beer for me in one hand, and what looks like soda for himself in the other. He leans in to speak, like he's trying to keep it private from my table.

"I'm really glad to see you here." His cologne smells nice, like cedar and soap, although it's mixed with the smell of cigarette smoke.

I look up at him. He not super tall, just tall enough for me to have to look up to talk to him. All I can do is smile and nod. I'm not sure how to reply.

He smiles and hands me the beer.

"See you later." He winks as he walks back towards a table full of the other band mates, along with others. A pair of beautiful women walk up to the table, one putting her hand on Samuel's arm as she whispers something to him.

"See?" I look and Noah and Olivia. "Not into me." I gesture my head to Samuel's table. Olivia rolls her eyes and laughs.

I hang around to finish the drink Samuel bought me and then say goodnight to Noah and Olivia. I'm exhausted and I need sleep, now. Noah and Olivia each pull me in for a hug and wish me a good night. I squeeze myself through the large groups of people to get to the front of the bar before I finally make it outside. I start to walk towards the direction of my apartment when I hear someone leave the bar after me.

"Payton!" Sam yells after me. I stop and turn around. "Heading home?" he says with a nervous smile as his hair rests over his forehead.

"Oh, um, yeah. I'm pretty exhausted." I shrug, pulling my arms closer to my side in a shudder. It's gotten very cold since I walked here a few hours ago.

Sam takes his leather jacket off and holds it out to me.

I put my hands up.

"Oh no, Samuel, you don't have to do that. Really. I'll be fine," I insist.

"Payton, I promise I don't do anything because I feel I have to. I want to, really." He holds out his jacket again. "Plus, you can give it back at the end of our walk." He smiles.

"Our walk?" I question him.

"Yeah, after I walk you home." He laughs.

"Oh really, I'll be okay, you don't have—" Samuel cuts me off.

"I'm sure you will, but I want to. Please." He laughs. "If you'll have me, of course," he says holding his jacket out for the third time. "Now please, put this on. You look freezing."

"What about your company?" I ask.

"What company?" He looks confused.

"Um, the woman you were with." I feel silly bringing it up.

He laughs, "Definitely not *my* company."

"Oh." She looked awfully friendly for someone he doesn't consider company.

"Interesting thing to notice tho." He winks. "Now... please," he says with a smile while holding out his jacket once again.

I playfully roll my eyes but accept his offer with a smile. I really am freezing and will take the added layer. The black jacket I wore was not nearly thick enough for how cold it has gotten. His jacket smells like his cedar cologne and leather mixed together.

Samuel holds his arm out in the direction of my apartment, "Shall we?" I nod and we begin to walk slowly, like before.

"You can call me Sam, ya know," he says after a few moments of silence.

"Oh, do you prefer Sam?" I ask and look at him. I pull his jacket tighter around me as the wind picks up.

"I mean, I don't mind either. 'Sam' is usually easier for people." He shrugs.

"Oh… well I like Samuel, if that's okay." I smile at him.

He looks at me and smiles with his hands in his pockets as we walk.

"Well, then call me Samuel," he says softly. His head is down but I can hear his smile.

As we walk, I found out he's been playing with his band for two years. He plays at a few different pubs about three days a week.

"It's really just a hobby. I'd love to make it big, of course. But those odds are so small. Plus, I have the bookstore to worry about."

I pause. "The bookstore?"

"Yeah," he sighs. "It was my dad's. He spent every minute of every day there. It was his pride and joy. And when he passed, he, uh, left it to me." He kicks a loose rock with his boots.

"Oh, when did he pass?" I ask, realizing that may be a bit too personal.

"Two years ago," he offers. "At first I had no idea what I was doing. I was going to sell the damn place and move on. But my sister convinced me to keep it going." As he speaks of his sister, I remember the kind girl behind the counter I met during one of my visits. I realize now that they look very alike.

"I'm glad she convinced you to keep it," I reply before I realize what I'm saying.

We stop in front of my apartment.

"Oh yeah?" he asks with a smile.

"Um, yeah. I guess." I smile as I remove his jacket and hold it out to him.

He holds his hand up. "Nope, you hold onto it."

"What?!" My eyes widen. "There's no way I can keep your leather jacket. Please," I beg as I hold his jacket out.

He laughs. "No, not keep. Just hold onto it. Bring it to the bookstore tomorrow."

"Why?" I question, bringing the jacket closer to me.

He shrugs. "Because then you'll have to come back to see me." He smiles at me through his dark hair that's falling onto his forehead. My stomach flutters.

I laugh. "I mean, I still have to bring back that book."

"Are you finished with it?" he asks.

"Um, not yet. Work has been cutting into my reading time." I laugh softly.

"Then that's why." He smiles, shyly looking down at the concrete.

"Samuel…" I say softly and before I can say anything else, he nods his head and starts to walk back towards the bar. Just as before, he glances back at me with a smile to see me watching him walk away.

I walk back into the apartment holding his jacket. I can't help but appreciate the smell of his cologne around the collar. I look at it for a moment and realize how long he must have had it. The jacket definitely shows some wear and tear. I hang it up on the hook next to the front door and walk straight towards the stairs. Between the loud music and alcohol, it's brought on a bit of a headache and I am ready for bed.

I walk into the bathroom and get ready for bed. The sink hardly offers any warm water so I wash my face as quickly as I can. I throw my hair into a high messy bun, brush my teeth, and walk over to bed.

I crawl under the sheets and find myself shifting around unable to get comfortable. After a few minutes of struggle, I pull out my phone and aimlessly scroll until my eyes start to feel heavy and I finally drift off to sleep.

Chapter Seven

The next morning comes too quickly as I'm woken up by the bright sun shining into my bedroom. I check the time: ten a.m. I can't remember the last time I slept in this late. I must have really needed it.

I get out of bed and jump into the shower. I smell of beer and cigarettes after being in that pub all night. The shower never once offered warm water this morning, so I make it extra fast.

I step out of the shower and blow-dry my hair. I place a few curls at the bottom and pin half of it up. I keep my make-up simple by just putting some mascara on. I'm very blonde, so without mascara, I practically look like I'm missing eyelashes.

I walk over to my closet and pull out the first T-shirt I see, a black V-neck, and put that on. Then I grab a pair of dark blue jeans. I give myself another look in the mirror feeling very… nervous. I have to bring Samuel's jacket back.

I walk downstairs, grab my bag, and slip my Converse sneakers on. I look at the book and contemplate bringing that back as well, seeing as I've already read it once before. But then I remember Samuel insisting that he get two visits out of me by having me bring back his jacket. And if I'm being honest with myself, I wouldn't made having multiple excuses to go back to the bookstore.

I grab his jacket and drape it over my arm. I can still smell his cologne lingering on the jacket. I swing my bag over my shoulder and head out of the apartment.

I find myself walking a little slower this time. Typically, the bookstore is only a ten- or fifteen-minute walk, but today it took me twenty minutes. I think my nerves slowed my pace.

I walk into the bookstore, hearing the bells echo throughout the store announcing my arrival. I look around for a moment when I hear someone come from the back.

The woman I saw before, whom I now assume is Samuel's sister, approaches the counter. She has dark-hair just like him and beautiful fair skin.

"Hi! Can I help you?" she asks, then looks down at the jacket in my arms and looks confused at first, then she smiles like she knows something I don't.

"Oh um, is Samuel here?" I ask. I can feel my face flush.

"No, he's not, I'm sorry. Is there something I can help you with?" she asks, glancing at the jacket.

"Um, if you just don't mind returning this to him," I say as I hold out the jacket, feeling disappointed.

"If you'd like to wait, he just stepped out to grab breakfast. He should be back any minute," she says with a smile.

But this is awkward enough already, "No that's okay. But thank you." I lay the jacket across the glass counter. Samuel's sister nods and grabs the jacket, disappearing into the back room.

I turn to leave the bookstore and just as I walk out, I run into Samuel, literally, making him drop a bag full of muffins on the ground.

I cover my mouth with my hands.

"Oh my God! I am so sorry!" Good job Payton.

He laughs.

"Please, don't worry about it. It was an accident." He looks at me and smiles. I help him pick up the now ruined muffins as we gather them back into the bag and toss them in the nearest garbage.

"I really am so sorry." My cheeks flush.

"Payton, it's okay," he says with a laugh. "It was nobody's fault." He scans my hands, and I know what he's looking for. His smile fades.

"Um, I left it with your sister. She said you weren't here." I shift uncomfortably.

"Oh," He looks disappointed. "Yeah sure, no problem." He shrugs and goes to walk inside.

"Wait," I say before my mind can catch up with my mouth. "Um, I feel like I owe you some muffins."

"It's okay Payton, really," he says as he turns to me, missing his signature smile.

"Well, I'm not offering because I feel like I have to, I'm offering because I want to." I smile, remembering his statement from last night.

He laughs and runs his fingers through his hair, "Well, I can't really argue that, now can I?"

"Nope." I smile. "Would you like to join me? To, ya know, pick your flavors and stuff," I ask as I shift back and forth on my feet.

"Are you sure?" he asks.

"Yeah, I am." I offer a warm smile.

He accepts my offer and starts walking in the direction of the bakery. It's just a few doors down and we don't say much on the journey.

We walk in and the smells of fresh baked goods fills my nose. It smells incredible in here. Samuel makes his order and explains to the cashier why he is back so soon while nudging me with his elbow. They laugh, I blush.

We head back towards the bookstore with little conversation between us. It feels strange. Once we get to the bookstore, he goes to walk inside but stops at the door and turns to me.

"Can I ask you something?" he says quietly.

My stomach drops, "Um sure," I reply.

"Why didn't you wait?" His cheeks flush, embarrassed by his own question.

"Um, wait for what?" I ask, knowing exactly what he means.

"For me to come back. To drop off the jacket, I mean." He sounds disappointed.

"Oh, um, I don't know. I'm guess I'm just not great with this sort of thing." I shift uncomfortably.

"What thing?" he asks.

Now I really feel stupid. Of course, he doesn't like me. I feel my cheeks turn bright red.

"Um, I don't… I don't know." I stutter, feeling my embarrassment heat my entire body.

"You're not great at what? Having a guy be into you?" he says with a laugh as he lifts one eyebrow at me.

I sigh, "Yeah, that, I guess." I smile with relief that I didn't make a total fool out of myself.

"Well, I am. Into you that is. And I'd really like to spend more time with you," he says, like he's been holding his breath for the last twenty minutes.

My face flushes once again and my stomach flutters. For someone with such a tough exterior, he speaks so gently and kind.

Just as I go to say yes, his face flashes in my mind. *His* face. I feel myself stiffen up and I briefly relive some of my most terrifying moments. The fear, the fights, the screaming. My hands ball into a fist.

"Payton?" Samuel asks, pulling me from my dark thoughts.

I look up at him, "Um, I don't know. There's just… I'm a…" I find myself scrambling to put a sentence together.

His face turns red.

"It's okay. Don't worry about it." He puts his hand through his hair and turns to walk back inside.

While my mind is still fuzzy, my mouth is clear on what it wants.

"Samuel, wait."

He turns back around and looks at me through the hair that's fallen back on his forehead.

"I have a lot of… baggage. There's just a lot that I'm…" I can't even finish the sentence.

"Payton, I'm just asking to spend some time with you. Not for your hand in marriage." He laughs nervously. My face flushes bright red but I can't help but laugh.

"Um, okay then," I agree.

"I mean, it's okay, really, if you don't want to. Please, don't do me any favors." He looks down at the concrete beneath us.

"Samuel, I'd like to. Really," I say with as much honestly as I can.

He sighs and after a few moments he smiles at me. "Are you free now?" he asks.

I gulp, "Now? Like right now?" My eyebrows rise.

He laughs, "Yes, like right now. Unless you have plans." He shoves his hands into his pocket.

"Um, no." I pause. "Like, no I don't have plans." I laugh. But then I remember, "Don't you have to be here?" I ask as I point to the bookstore.

"Sarah's got it." He winks. "Just give me a minute," he says as he walks back inside with the muffins. After a few minutes he walks back outside with two muffins in his hands.

"Ready?" he asks. "I've got an idea," he says as he hands me a muffin, lemon poppyseed… my favorite.

Chapter Eight

He begins to walk down the road and I follow. He has a white shirt on, and with the sunshining down, it's thin enough to see through to the black markings covering his body. I have a few small tattoos, but he is covered. He has one that peaks out from his shirt collar, and many more that span the length of his arms. As he pushes his hair back, I see a small one placed behind his ear, a dagger.

We walk slowly as we pick at our muffins. His looks like blueberry. He breaks it off with his fingers, which are weighted with his heavy silver rings and tosses a piece into his mouth.

"So, um, where are we going?" I ask, to break the silence.

"It's a surprise." He looks over at me and winks.

I pull my bottom lip between my teeth and nod. He takes a sharp breath and pulls his eyes away from me.

We continue to walk with small banter between us. He talks about his sister being in college and how she wants to become a nurse. I told him about my new job at the diner and how I met Noah and Olivia. Talking to Samuel is surprisingly easy and the conversation flows naturally.

After about fifteen minutes of walking, we arrive at a beautiful white house. Each window adorned with an arch. It's incredible.

"This is the Keats House." Samuel begins to explain, "The poet, John Keats, lived here. Now it's a literary museum. You haven't been here long, so I assumed you haven't been. And being into books and all…"

I stare at the house in amazement.

"Um, unless you have. Or don't care for this stuff, then we can do something else," he continues.

"No, I haven't been, actually. It's beautiful." I look at him and we both smile.

"Great, then let's head in then, shall we?" He places his hand on the small of my back and walks with me inside.

We go from room to room, admiring each artifact and talking about how this place looks untouched from when John Keats left, in 1820. We read the small descriptions that come with each room. Samuel's hand brushes mine a few times. Accident or not, the contact sends shock waves up my arm. In one room, he grabbed my hand to pull me over to admire a poem written in a journal beneath a glass case. His hand held mine for just a moment before letting go.

We made our way through the museum in an hour. As we step outside, I am happy to see the sunshine decided to stick around. Gloomy cloudy days are sort of a regular here.

"Well, I'm starving, how 'bout you?" he asks, rubbing his hands together.

"Yeah, I could definitely go for some lunch." All I ate this morning was the small muffin Samuel gave me.

"There's a small take-out place right up the road here," he says. I nod and begin to follow him.

We walk up to the counter and I order a water with a chicken salad and Samuel orders a soda with a burger.

"Aren't Europeans known for having alcohol with every meal or something?" I joke.

He smiles and looks at his hands, "Yeah maybe. Just not me I guess." I can tell there's more to that statement, but I don't push.

We gather our food and walk over to a grassy area nearby. Samuel walks over to a large hill and nods to me. We sit on the grass, close enough for our knees to touch every so often.

"So, are you gonna tell me the real reason you came all the way to England by yourself?" He looks at me.

I pause, unsure of how to reply. "Um, we'll see. Someday, maybe," I say, trying to keep the conversation moving.

"Sorry." He flushes after seeing my discomfort. "I don't mean to pry or be nosey."

"Yeah, you do," I say playfully, "but it's okay." I offer him a smile to reassure him.

He laughs softly. "Yeah you're right. I just really want to know more about you."

The conversation stays light through lunch as he tells me about his band playing at another pub this evening. He invites me to go but I explain that I have the morning shift at work tomorrow and should probably call it an early night. He looks disappointed but nods as he finishes the last few bites of his burger.

We both finish up our food and sit in the sunshine for a moment longer.

"I'm really glad we did this," he says with a wide smile, resting his hands on his knees.

"Yeah, me too." I smile.

"I hope there's more in the future," he replies, but it sounds more like a question. I turn and nod with a smile.

He sighs. "Oh, um, great." He smiles nervously. "I should get going, I guess. We got a shipment today and Sarah's not one for heavy lifting." He laughs and stands up, turning around to help me up. We stand face to face, not moving for just a moment, before he smiles and turns to walk back to the bookstore.

We return to the bookstore and stop in front of the door. Samuel could tell I was a little cold, so he walked pretty close to me the entire walk back. Despite the sunshine, the wind started to pick up.

"I had a really nice time." He smiles at me.

"Yeah, I did too." I smile and shift uncomfortably.

Before I even realized what was happening, Samuel leans in and plants a soft kiss on my cheek. His lips are much softer than I would have expected.

"Um, sorry," he says, realizing he caught me by surprise.

"No." I look at his dark, almost black, eyes. "Don't be." I smile at him and he smiles back.

"So, I'll, uh, see you next time," he stammers. I nod. He walks into the bookstore. I turn and before I even have a chance to take a step, I hear the bells on the door. I turn back around, and Samuel is standing in the doorway with his leather jacket in his hand.

"Here." He smiles as he holds out his jacket.

I sigh, but I don't argue this time. I take his jacket and slip my arms in, wrapping the heavy material around me. I nod and begin walking back towards my apartment inhaling the intoxicating smell of cedar and leather.

Chapter Nine

The next two days go by in a blink. I worked morning shifts both days at work, and it was super busy. I dropped a tray full of drinks on my shoes; a screaming young boy threw his pasta on my pants, and I'm pretty sure I'm the slowest waitress there. But Laura and the rest of my coworkers were so kind and made sure I left feeling like I did the best I could. Food service workers really deserve more credit.

During my two days of work, I kept replaying my time with Samuel in my mind. I had such a great time with him. But in between positive memories flashed horrible ones. Ones I've worked so hard to forget. I tried to shake them from my head, but they always come back. I know Samuel's not like that, I think. I'm sure he would never do things like that. But I never thought *he* would do them either. And I if I'm being honest with myself, I really don't know Samuel. At all.

I get off work at five p.m. I'm exhausted and ready to take a hot shower and crawl into bed. I finished rereading *The Great Gatsby*, finally, and plan to stop at the bookstore to drop it off. I wish I didn't look like I just worked one of my hardest shifts so far, but it's been a couple days since I've seen or talked to Samuel and I'd really like to stop by.

I step into the bookstore and the bell goes off, alerting the store that I'm here. I walk up to the countertop and wait. A few minutes go by and I'm so distracted by the new pile of books on the counter that I didn't even notice Samuel behind the counter.

"Um, earth to Payton?" He laughs and I look up at him.

"Oh, hey. Sorry, I noticed you added some new ones to the pile." I place his book on the counter.

"Did you like it?" he asks softy, waiting for my opinion.

"Yeah, I did. Definitely one of my better reads." I smile.

I read through the new book descriptions when he interrupts me.

"Hm, convincing," he smirks.

I smile back. "I'm sorry, work was... well it was something else today."

"Well, um, I was thinking..." He pauses and I look up at him. "Do you, uh, have plans tonight?" He eagerly waits for my response.

I begin to think of my plans that involve taking a hot shower and crawling into bed before eight p.m. Then I look at Samuel and the hope his eyes have.

"Uh, no not really." I chuckle. "Why, what's up?" I ask nervously.

"Well, I would like to maybe do dinner?" It comes out as more of a question than a statement. He looks up at me through his hair.

"Um, yeah. Sure." I shrug. My relaxing plans dissolve in my mind, but I'm not necessarily sad about it.

"Awesome, great." He lets out the breath he was holding. "Would you mind meeting me back here, around eight p.m.?" he asks, hopeful.

"Sure," I reply with a warm smile. People on this side of the world have dinner so much later than I'm used to. We both nod to one another as I turn and leave. I need to get home and shower the diner grease out of my hair.

I arrive at my apartment and go straight upstairs to the shower. I don't even stop to remove my shoes at the door. I undress and am amazed when the shower is perfectly hot, relaxing each and every muscle underneath my skin. I step out, dry off, and blow-dry my hair. I throw in a couple curls in an attempt to look decent. I pull half of it up and allow my bangs to fall around my face. I add a little bit of mascara and walk over to the closet to get dressed. He didn't exactly tell me where we are going. I'm not sure what Samuel's idea of a dinner date is, but I could only assume it's probably some pub with loud music. So, I grab a white T-shirt and throw on my black jeans and my black boots. I check the mirror one last time and decide I'm too exhausted to put in much more effort than I already have. I head downstairs and grab Samuel's leather jacket off the hook by the front door. I throw it on to keep myself warm on the way there and grab my thinner black jacket and throw it in my bag to wear home tonight.

I head down the road towards the bookstore. My nerves are starting to kick in now. I think I was so exhausted earlier that my brain had no extra energy to really process what he had asked me. He wants to have dinner, with me. And why are we meeting at the bookstore? Why not meet at the pub, or wherever it is we're going?

My nerves had me practically sprinting there so my walk only takes ten minutes, and I'm ten minutes early. I see a big *'Closed'* sign on the door and the lights look off besides a soft glow coming from the center of the store. I try the door and it opens. The bells chime as I walk in.

As soon as I close the door behind me, Samuel appears from the back room behind the counter. His hair is neater than usual, but he still swipes his hand through it out of habit. He's wearing the same black short sleeved button up I saw him in the first day I visited the bookstore, but today its tucked into his black jeans. They have a rip in each knee and end with a pair of black Converses. I see more black markings poke through the tears in his jeans. His nails have a fresh coat of black polish on them and his fingers have their normal row of thick silver rings. His neck has one single necklace, the chunky silver one with a small lock on it. I hear faint music from somewhere in the store playing a mild-tempo indie playlist.

"Payton, I'm really glad you're here." He smiles.

"Yeah, me too." I walk towards the counter. "So, where are we going to eat? The pub? Anywhere but the diner I hope." I laugh. It's been a while since I've eaten and I'm pretty hungry.

"Um, actually, I was thinking we could eat here. If that's okay." His nerves are becoming increasingly obvious, it's endearing.

"Um, sure. Are we going to order take out?" I ask, not really sure where he's suggesting.

"Actually, I already took care of it." He smiles and runs his hands through his hair.

I'm confused, "Wait, what?" I ask.

"Follow me." He winks as he comes from around the counter and holds his hand out. I give a small smile and place my hand in his. "By the way, nice jacket." He brings one corner of his mouth up into a half-smile.

He takes me through a few aisles of books and stops at a large opening in the middle of the bookstore. I look around and see a small table in the center with two plates of pasta, two glasses of water, and a single wine glass. I notice a bottle of wine placed on ice in a rusty grey bucket on the floor next to the table. String lights are spread over the bookshelves surrounding us, along with some candles placed on top of the short shelves. I feel like I just walked into *Lady & the Tramp*.

"Oh… wow." My jaw drops.

"I know it's probably too much and way too cheesy for a second date. But my sister convinced me this would be a good idea." He looks at me waiting for my approval.

Is it too much? Probably. Cheesy? Definitely. But also, the kindest thing anyone has done for me in a long time.

I look at Samuel, who's eagerly awaiting my response.

"No, it's… it's perfect." He smiles and lets out a deep sigh of relief. He helps me out of my… well, *his* jacket, and places it on the back of my chair as he pulls out the chair for me. He sits down across from me and takes a sip of his water. He grabs the wine bottle, pops it open and pours me a glass.

"Um, thank you," I say after I take a sip. "Are you not having any?" I ask, noticing he doesn't have a wine glass in front of him.

"No, I'll stick to water." He smiles as he begins to eat his pasta.

I take a few bites of mine and realize this pasta is amazing.

"Oh my God, where did you get this.?" I ask, with a mouthful of pasta.

His eyes get wide, "Uh, why?" he asks nervously.

"Because it's amazing. Honestly. It's so good," I add as I take a few more bites.

He looks relieved and smiles. "Well, I made it. My sister helped, of course, but it was mostly me," he says with a wink.

We go on through dinner and I'm on my second glass of wine. We talk of our favorite books and books we read as kids. I go through the books I've read since arriving. He tells me stories of how his dad used to read to him as a kid.

His eyes light up when he tells stories of his dad. He describes them as best friends. As he continues to talk of his dad, I notice his eyes become sad. I distract him by changing the subject to his sister and how they grew up together. He tells me story after story of how they would prank each other as children. He tells me one story about how he got in big trouble once when he put a frog under his sisters' pillow. We are laughing so hard my stomach hurts and he wipes tears from his eyes.

Our laughter eventually fades, and we sit in a comfortable silence. He studies me from across the table.

I look around to all the bookshelves and begin to feel more confident than I should.

"Will you… will you read to me?" I ask, then freeze. I cannot believe I just asked him that. Clearly, I've had enough wine.

"Um, yeah, of course. What would you like me to read?" he asks quietly, stammering a bit. I clearly surprised him with my question as much as I did myself.

I ponder the question for a moment, then decide "Something from *The Great Gatsby*. A few favorite quotes maybe?"

He smiles as he stands up and walks over to one of the many bookshelves surrounding us. He spends a moment searching before grabbing the book from the shelf. He stares at the cover and runs his thumb through the pages.

"Now, what to choose?" He looks over at me. I can barely see him in the dim lighting, made only darker by the bookshelf he's standing by. But I see the shine from his rings and the smile on his face. He walks over and goes to sit back at the table.

"How about we read over there?" I point to a spot on the floor where the light is decent enough to read.

"Um, yeah. Sure." He wipes his hands on his pants. I'm assuming his nerves are making his palms sweat, because mine are doing the same. He grabs the book and meets me on the floor with our back against another bookshelf.

"Are you sure you're comfortable?" he asks and I shift back and forth. I nod and smile.

He begins to search through the book before settling on a page.

"'He stretched out his arms toward the dark water in a curious way, and far as I was from him, I could have sworn he was trembling. Involuntarily I glanced seaward — and distinguished nothing except a single green light, minute and far away. When I looked once more for Gatsby he had vanished, and I was alone again in the unquiet darkness.'"

He looks over at me as if he's waiting for my permission to continue. I nod to him and offer a smile. He begins again on another page.

"'And what's more, I love Daisy too. Once in a while I go off on a spree and make a fool of myself, but I always come back, and in my heart I love her all the time.'"

The quotes are beautiful, and his accent makes them sound even more sweet than they already are. He reads them slowly, with purpose. I move a bit closer, our shoulders meeting. It sends an electrical signal down my entire body and my heart rate begins to pick up.

He flips to the next page when he pushes his hair back and I notice the dagger tattoo I saw before.

"What does this tattoo mean?" I ask as I touch the tattoo lightly with my index finger. I'm surprised by my own brazenness. I watch his neck fill with goosebumps.

"Um, I got it to remind me of a… quote," he replies as he runs his finger behind his ear, over the tattoo.

"What quote?" The words just keep dropping from my wine-induced mouth.

He shifts uncomfortably. "Um." He clears his throat. "'You pierce my soul. I am half agony, half hope.' It's um, Jane Austen."

"Oh." I sense his discomfort and don't push any further. We sit in silence for just a moment.

"It's a saying my girlfriend and I used to say to each other." He looks over at me, his eyes dark.

My eyes widen, "Girlfriend?" I ask as I lean away, slightly.

He laughs. "Well, obviously not a current girlfriend." He smiles down at the book of poems still in his hands.

"Oh, so ex-girlfriend?" My demeanor softens.

"Yeah, I guess. Kind of." He shifts, looking uncomfortable. "She, uh, died." He looks down and runs his thumb over the cover of the book.

"Oh, I'm sorry. I don't mean to…" My face flushes.

"No, it's okay." He looks back up at me. "Her name was Allison. We were together for years, since we were kids, really." He smiles at mention of her name.

"What happened? If you don't mind." Did I really just ask that? What is wrong with me?

"Um, as we got older… we started hanging around a not so good group of folks. We were doing things we shouldn't have and… she overdosed." My jaw felt like it actually hit the floor this time.

He continues, "I was there… when it happened, and I called the Emergency line. But by the time they got there she was already gone. I was high and didn't know what else to do… so I ran. And I kept running until I physically couldn't." He rubs his hand on the back of his neck. As he tells me this story I remember back to when Olivia mentioned that she had heard rumors that he doesn't hang out with the best people.

"I'm… I'm so sorry." I place my hand on his arm.

"Thanks." He shrugs. "It's been three years. It gets easier every day. I guess." He smiles as he looks down at my hand on his arm.

"Is that why you don't drink?" Wow. My word vomit never seems to stop. No more wine for me tonight.

"Um, kind of, yeah." He starts to spin the rings on his fingers. After a moment of awkward silence, I hear one of my favorite songs come across the speakers and an opportunity to change the mood.

"Oh my God, I love this song," I say as I close my eyes to listen, my hand still on him.

"Really?" He smiles and he stands up. He walks over to the speaker and turns it up. He walks back over to me and holds out his hand. I look up at him.

"May I have this dance?" he says, holding back a smile.

I smile and roll my eyes as he pulls me off the floor and into his chest. He places one arm at the small of my back and takes my other hand in his, holding it close to us. I can smell mint on his breath mixed with his cologne and together it creates my new favorite scent.

He rocks slowly as I close my eyes to listen. He surprises me with a sudden dip as I let out a loud laugh. He pulls me back close to him, laughing with me, and moves gently from side to side.

I clear my throat and try to embrace the confidence the wine has graced me with.

"So, have you had any other girlfriends since Allison?"

I swallow hard, unsure if I want to know the answer.

"Um, no, actually. I, uh, haven't even been on a date really. Well, until now of course." He lets out a small laugh.

I look at him, my eyes wide.

"What?" I need him to repeat that.

He looks down at me.

"You're the first person I've had a date with since Allison."

I stop moving but keep our embrace.

"Why?" I pause. "Why me?" I ask softly.

He pauses and thinks, then he smiles, "There's just… something about you. Can't put my finger on it."

I've lost track of time at this point. I smile and lay my head on his chest as he begins to shift back and forth to the next song. I can hear his heartbeat. It feels like it's about to beat out of his chest, and I'm sure mine feels the same.

Once the next song is over, he stops moving. His heart is pounding even harder now. I lift my head off his chest and look at him. The light from the candle is flickering a warm glow off his face. I watch him scan my face and stop at my lips, then back to my eyes. My lips part as I take a deep breath in.

Understanding my invitation, he leans down, and our lips meet. They meet, but briefly. He pulls back and studies me for a moment. His one hand stays at the small of my back while his other hand drops mine and meets my cheek. His rings are cold to the touch. He runs his thumb along my cheek bone and smiles as he leans back down and kisses me again. This time, harder. I can taste the mint I smelled earlier. His hands are rough but kind. His lips are soft but forceful. His tongue separates my lips even further meeting his tongue to mine. The tense nervousness I was feeling all night has faded and all I feel is want. I relax in his arms as I move my hand to the back of his neck and run my fingers through his shaggy hair and gently grasp a handful. I hear a small moan leave his mouth into mine. I feel goosebumps cover my entire body.

After a few minutes, though it felt like a few seconds, he pulls away keeping his forehead connected to mine.

71

Both of us nearly gasping for breath. I can see him smile in the flickering candlelight. He lifts his head off mine, leaving his hand on my neck, stroking my jawline with his thumb, and watching my movements.

No words are spoken as the next song begins to play over the speakers. He pulls me back to his chest and places his one hand at the small of my back and grabs my other hand in his. We begin to dance again. I look up at him and he smiles down at me. He plants a small kiss in the center of my forehead and touches his forehead back to mine. I couldn't keep track of how many songs we danced through. We may have been there for an hour or four. Either way I wouldn't be able to tell the difference, nor do I care. Samuel's touch is so comforting and gives me a feeling of safety and shelter. A feeling I have been searching for, for so long.

Chapter Ten

We sway back and forth for another few songs, no words between us. We don't need words. I can feel everything he would want to say. I lift my head and glance at the clock on the wall behind Samuel.

I gasp. "Oh my God. It's already two a.m." I look up at Samuel. He turns and looks at the clock.

"Wow, yeah I guess it is," he says with a rasp to his voice.

"I better go, I guess," I say, wishing I could stay here and dance all night. But the exhaustion from work is starting to creep back into my sore body.

"Yeah, of course." He smiles. "I'll grab my jacket and I'll walk you home." He smiles and turns to grab the leather jacket off the chair. He holds it out to me.

I laugh and don't bother to fight him. I grab the jacket and wrap it around myself.

We walk out the front door of the bookstore and I wait as Samuel locks the door with what look like janitor keys. There has to be fifty keys on that keyring.

He turns back to me.

"Shall we?" He smiles as he holds his arm out in the direction of my apartment. I nod and begin to walk beside him.

The walk is quiet, but not awkward or uncomfortable. Samuel walks with his hands in his front pockets and glances over at me.

"I, uh, had a really nice time," I say, breaking the silence between us.

He smiles, "Yeah, me too. I know it was probably a bit over the top, but it's been a while since I've... well you know." He laughs and shrugs his shoulders.

I playfully bump my shoulder into his.

"No, it was perfect. It really was."

He laughs and rolls his eyes.

"You're very polite," he says as he laughs.

He takes his hands out of his pockets and walks with them at his sides. His knuckles brushing against mine. I smile and uncurl my fingers tapping my ring finger to his. He laughs softly and slides my hand into his and laces our fingers together.

We walk hand in hand without much conversation. But it's a comfortable silence. His thumb rubs over mine and I tighten my grip on his hand.

We arrive at my apartment and our hands separate. I turn to him and remove the leather jacket.

He holds his hands up. "Hang on to it for me." He smiles.

"Samuel, it's freezing out here. Please, take it." I hold it out and he pauses. I can practically see his breath it's so cold out. "I promise, I don't need an excuse to come to the bookstore. Seeing you will be the only excuse I need." I laugh and hold out his jacket once again.

He laughs and runs his hands through his hair. He grabs the jacket from me and wraps it around himself.

He pauses for a moment, "Well, um, goodnight... Payton." He smiles and studies my face.

"Goodnight," I return, waiting. I'm not sure what I'm waiting for, but I'm waiting for something. Anything.

He takes a step towards me locking into my eyes. He leans into me and places a kiss on my cheek. He leans back up and goes to turn around as I grab his arm. He turns towards me looking confused. I take a step into him with my hand still on his arm, keeping eye contact and place my other hand behind his head and wrap my fingers into his dark hair. He smiles and grabs me by my waist and pulls me in closer. He pauses a moment before bringing his lips to mine. I feel his hair fall onto his forehead and brush against mine. The kiss is tender, soft, and not nearly long enough.

He pulls back, leaving our foreheads connected.

He sighs.

"I really like you Payton." His eyes are closed. I nod against him, holding our connection. His eyes flutter open and look into mine.

"Okay." He stands up straight, letting me go. "If I don't leave now, I'm not going to." He laughs. "So, I'll, um, see you soon?" he asks. I nod at him and smile, shoving my hands into my jean pockets. He nods as he turns away and starts to walk back towards the bookstore. I swear, sometimes I think he lives there. He gets about twenty steps away before he turns and glances in my direction. Even from this far, I can see him smile as I watch him walk away.

I shuffle through my bag and find the keys to my apartment. I open the door and walk inside, quietly closing the door behind me. I put my back against the door and rest my head back while I process the incredible evening I just had. I touch my cheek and I can still feel his hand caressing my face as he pulled me deeper into his mouth. My skin fills with goosebumps at the memory. I recall how soft his lips were as I run my index finger across my bottom lip. Who would have thought the man covered in tattoos and cold jewelry would be so kind and comforting? Such a rough exterior to a warm kind-hearted person.

I break from my trance and walk upstairs. I change from my jeans into my warm pajama pants. I go to remove my T-shirt until I smell a familiar smell on it: cedar. His cologne must have rubbed off on my shirt as we were dancing. I decide to keep the shirt on and wear it to bed, allowing the memory of the evening to lull me to sleep. I crawl into bed, pulling the covers up to my ears. The apartment gets very cold at night. I slowly begin to drift off to sleep with visions of flickering candlelight taking over my mind.

Chapter Eleven

The glass shatters next to my head against the headboard. I tighten my eyes and pull the covers over my head.

"I do everything for you!" he screams. I hear his footsteps reach the bed as he pulls the covers off me. I look at him, trying to speak but I can't. I sit up and shuffle myself towards the wall the bed sits against. I tuck my knees into my chest, still trying to scream with no success. He looks at me with tears in his eyes, sadness mixed with anger. He grabs my wrist and tries to pull me towards him. I stiffen and try my best to pull myself away, but he's stronger. Much stronger. His grip is so tight my hand starts to turn white, then purple. I look into his eyes and his pupils have taken over, making his eyes look almost completely black. I struggle underneath his grip trying to pull myself free. "All I do is try to be better for you," he growls. "I love you. I need to show you that I love you."

I shake my head; all I can do is cry. The harder I fight his grip the more painful it becomes.

"Stop!" I scream as I shoot up in bed. The word felt like vomit as it left my mouth. I look around into my apartment, lit by the sunrise outside. My heart is racing, and my face is drenched. I tuck my knees to my chest and begin to sob. When will these nightmares end? Will they ever?

As I sob into my knees with my hands wrapped around my legs, I smell Samuel's cologne that lingers on the shirt I'm wearing. I touch my nose to my shoulder and breathe in the comforting scent. My breath begins to slow, as well as the tears. I look at the time on my phone and it's only six a.m.. I'm on about three hours of terrible sleep, but I know there is no point in trying to go back sleep. I get up and walk into the bathroom.

I turn on the sink and splash ice-cold water onto my face in an attempt to wake myself up and rinse the mix of sweat and tears off my cheeks. I look into the mirror and notice the dark puffy circles forming under my eyes.

I throw my hair into a high bun and grab my running clothes from the top of the hamper. I really need to do laundry.

I step into the leggings and pull on my sports bra. I place my pajama pants on the hamper, and I go to do the same with my white shirt that I wore to bed, but I pause. I hold the white shirt in my hand for a moment before I bring it up to my face to inhale the cedar scent. I walk out of the bathroom, shirt in hand, and toss it onto the bed.

I grab my headphones and pop them into each ear and play my playlist of high-tempo songs for my run. I jog down the stairs of my apartment and head outside.

My feet are hitting the pavement. The weather is brisk and burns my lungs as I breath in and out. As my usual escape, my run is not offering the expected relief this morning, so I turn my music up even higher. As my mind still involuntarily plays the nightmare in my head over and over, I close my eyes and begin to run faster down the straight path. My eyes are closed for only a moment and when I open them, I'm brought to a halt. I'm only a few stores away from the coffee shop when I see Samuel on the sidewalk looking over at me. He smiles and waves as I begin to walk in his direction.

"Um, good morning," he laughs. "Didn't expect to see you around this early. Especially after um…" He clears his throat. "… our late night." He shoves his hands into his pockets as his face flushes. I've noticed that he does this when he's nervous.

"Um, I didn't sleep well," I reply as I walk up to him in front of the coffee shop.

"Oh?" he replies quizzically.

"What, uh, brings you here so early?" I ask in return.

"Um, I couldn't sleep either," he replies with a small smile.

Eager to change the subject, I point to the coffee shop, "Care to join me? It's kind of a post-run ritual I have."

I smile and walk into the coffee shop; Samuel nods and follows behind me.

I walk up and greet Noah with a nod and a smile. Noah looks at me, then at Samuel, then back at me. His eyes widen, along with his smile. I roll my eyes.

Noah clears his throat.

"So, the usual?" he asks, and I nod.

"And for your, uh, friend?" he says with a devious smile as he looks at Samuel.

"I'll take an English breakfast with a blueberry muffin." He goes to take out his wallet and I step in front of the counter.

I look back at Samuel.

"Absolutely not," I say with a laugh. He smiles and runs his hand through his hair, rolling his eyes.

"Fine," he growls. "But just this once."

I lead him over to my usual spot, right by the window. I take a moment to stare out at the streets, and admire the purple glow the sunrise brings.

"You must come here often." He clears his throat. "He knows your 'usual'?" he asks, but I can tell he's asking about something else.

"Um, yeah. That's Noah; I was at the pub with him and his girlfriend, Olivia, the night I saw you play," I explain, smiling, emphasizing 'girlfriend'.

His face softens. "Oh." And he smiles. "Sorry. I didn't recognize him."

I laugh as Noah brings us our orders and places them on the table. Noah glances over at me gives me a half-smile and as he turns back towards the coffee bar.

"So, why didn't you sleep well?" he asks as he sips his tea.

"Um, a nightmare."

I look down at my food. I shift in my seat and break off a piece of my scone, popping it into my mouth.

"A bad one?" he asks as he looks at me through his hair cupping his hands around his hot mug.

I drop the second piece of scone I broke off back onto the plate and sit back in my chair.

"Yeah," I sigh. "A bad one." I've suddenly lost my appetite.

He looks at me, sympathetically.

"Want to talk about it?"

His eyes are soft, and I hear the concern in his voice.

I force a smile and take a sip of my coffee. "No, not really," I reply softly.

"I'm sorry," he says as he looks down and breaks off a piece of his muffin.

"It's okay," I reply. "Running always helps clear my head." I shrug. "And I've been doing a lot of it lately."

He glances between me and his coffee. As he looks at me, I remember the story he shared with me about Allison. He was so vulnerable and shared intimate details of the worst day of his life. He trusted me and trusted that I would pass no judgement. I take a deep breath in, knowing it's only fair to share parts of me. Small parts, but parts, nonetheless.

I clear my throat.

"I have them once or twice a week," I offer.

His eyes meet mine, waiting for me to continue.

"And when I run, I feel like I can run from them. Although, today it was a little more difficult to outrun them."

I take a sip of my coffee.

"I don't mean to be crass, but maybe that's why you keep having them. Because you're running from them.

Instead of facing whatever it is that's…" He looks up at me and my face hardens. "Um, I'm sorry, it's really none of my business." He shifts uncomfortably in his seat.

I feel my mood change. And all I can think is, who the hell does he think he is? He has no idea what I have been through. Who is he to tell me I'm running from my problems? Is he saying I deserve to relive these nightmares over and over again? He knows nothing about me. I have no words. I can tell that he senses my mood change.

"Payton, I really am sorry. I didn't mean to—" He reaches out for my hand that's wrapped around my coffee.

"It's fine." I cut him off and move my hands to my lap. My mouth turns to a flat line and I honestly find it hard to even look at him. We sit in a very awkward silence for a moment. I feel a fire starting inside of me, and I can't sit here any longer. I look down, I've hardly touched my coffee or my scone, but I need to leave.

"Um, I should really go," I say as I stand. He stands with me.

"Please Payton, I'm really sorry. I had no right," he says and he grabs my wrist as I try to leave. The nightmare twists its way into my head, the vision of my hand turning purple plays in my mind. I jerk my arm out of his soft grip.

I look up at him, fighting back tears.

"You're right, you didn't. You know nothing about me," I say angrily as I turn and walk towards the door. I hear him call my name as I put my earphones back into my ears and begin to run back to my apartment. I've never run this fast in my life.

Chapter Twelve

I run up to my apartment door and place my hands on my knees. I ran back here so fast and I am completely out of breath. My lungs are burning, and my entire body feels like it's going to collapse. Samuel's words reply in my head and as slam my eyes shut and shake my head. I'm still mad, really mad.

After catching my breath, I walk into the apartment and go upstairs. I gather my clothes from the hamper and put them into a large bag to bring with me to the laundromat. I remove the sweat-soaked clothes I'm wearing and toss them into the bag as well. I jump into the shower, skipping my hair. I don't have the energy to blow-dry it today and it's too cold to leave it wet.

I get out of the shower and find the last clean shirt in my closet. It's an old band T-shirt with faded white lettering spelling *The Smiths: The Queen is Dead* with an image of the band members standing in front of a brick building. The shirt is so old and faded that it's barely black and is more of a dark grey color now. I tuck the shirt into my dark blue jeans. They're not exactly clean, but they'll have to wait until the next laundry day.

I spray what feels like a pound of dry shampoo through my hair and grab the laundry bag. As I walk pass the bed, I notice my white shirt lying on top of my sheets. I pause a moment before grabbing it off the bed. I bring it up to my face and inhale Samuel's scent. A few hours ago, the scent calmed me, but right now it just pisses me off, so I throw it into the bag with the rest of my clothing.

I arrive at the laundromat that's just across the street from the apartments. I pick the biggest washer and throw all of my clothes in at once. I've never been a 'light and dark cycle' kind of person. I start the machine and my stomach starts to growl. I took two bites of my scone at the coffee shop and never ate breakfast after I stormed out. I look around and see a rusty vending machine in the corner. I walk over and put in a few coins. The little package of chocolate donuts looks as appealing as vending machine snacks can get, so I press the corresponding numbers on the keypad. Once they fall, I grab my breakfast from the bottom tray and walk back over to the table near the washer.

Time feels like it's going backwards. Typically, I would have brought a book to read, but I never took a new one from the bookstore last time I was there.

I sigh and think about last night. I relive the incredible evening I had with Samuel. We laughed and talked for hours, even though it only felt like minutes. I picture him sitting across the table from me telling more stories about how he would prank his sister when they were younger. I look down and pick at my nails. I'm starting to feel bad.

Maybe I overreacted this morning. Okay, I definitely overreacted. The nightmare was still so fresh in my mind and his statement triggered something inside me. I moved halfway across the world in an attempt to escape the prison I was held in. I've shared nothing with no one and the first time I offer even a snippet of private information, he offers advice I didn't ask for. But I know that he didn't mean anything mean by it. Samuel is such a kind person, and I can tell that he really does care about me, not just romantically, but as a friend.

I watch the infomercial playing on the only television in the entire place and eat the rest of the mini donuts. The washer ends and I stand to place the wet clothes in the dryer. As I place each item in the dryer, I come across the white shirt that once held the scent of Samuel's cologne. I bring the shirt to my nose and am disappointed that the only smell it holds now is that of detergent. I toss it into the dryer with the rest of the clothing and start the cycle.

Time continues to stall as I watch the infomercials switch off and be replaced by a morning talk show. The dryer sounds off signaling that it's complete. I walk over and pull each item out, folding it, and placing it back into the bag as neatly as possible.

I leave the laundromat around eleven a.m. This is why I hate laundry days. I feel like I spend the entire day there. I usually don't mind it too much, when I have something to read, but today just felt like a waste of the morning. I start to think about stopping at the bookstore. I really do want to grab a new book, but I also want to see Samuel.

My stomach twists at the thought of how I treated him this morning. I was so abrupt and left him there at the coffee shop, alone.

I carry my large bag of clothes back into my apartment and begin to put them away. I usually don't put them away so soon. They usually sit in the bag as I pick through them for a day or so before I finally cave and put them away, but today I am definitely looking for a way to stall my bookstore visit. I try to think of what to say when I see Samuel. Do I apologize or wait for him to? Well, technically he already did apologize. And I basically told him to screw off.

I finish putting my clothes away and decide that I'll stop at the diner and pick up lunch, for two. Maybe if I bring him lunch, he'll forgive — or better yet, forget — my abrupt exit without me having to explain much. I look in the mirror and decide to put my hair back into a bun. The dry shampoo is making my hair look dry and helpless.

I go downstairs and slip on my black Converses and cuff my jeans at the bottom. The weather is cloudy, but warm. I grab my bag and walk towards the diner.

As I walk into the diner, I see Lily at the counter. The poor girl works too much. I usually work four days a week, but Lily is here almost every day. On my first day I learned she has three kids, all under ten, and their father is no longer around. She said he just decided one day that this wasn't the life he wanted, and he left. However, she still manages to be one of the sweetest women around, next to Laura of course.

"Good morning," I offer as I walk up to her. She looks over at me and offers a bright smile.

"Good morning!" she practically yells, "Can't get enough of this place, huh?" She laughs.

"Actually, I'd like to place a carry out," I explain as I scan the menu.

"Sure, what can I get ya?" she asks.

I'm not really sure what to get. All I've seen Samuel eat is a burger at lunch and pasta at dinner. Oh, and a blueberry muffin. I scan the menu and decide to keep it to what I know he'll eat. I order a chicken salad for me and a burger for Samuel.

"Will that be all?" Lily asks, clearly out of habit, as she laughs. I laugh with her and nod.

The food is done quickly and Lily brings it out me in a paper bag. I thank her as I hand her cash, giving her a little extra as a thank you. I grab the bag and walk out as Lily yells out, "See you tomorrow!" I smile and wave back as the door closes behind me.

I'm walking towards the bookstore and I can feel my nerves building inside of my stomach. My grip tightens around the handle of the brown paper bag and I start to doubt my decision. He probably doesn't want to see me again after this morning. I stop about five feet from the bookstore and then quickly turn around. This was stupid. This was a very stupid idea. What was I thinking?

As I go to walk away, I hear the bell chime on the door. I pause for a moment, then slowly turn around to see

Samuel standing at the door, looking at me with soft eyes as his hair rests on his forehead.

"Payton?" he asks quietly. He scans my face and glances down at the bag in my hand.

"Um, hi," I reply, my voice is harsh as my entire mouth has gone dry.

"Um, hi. Are you just passing by?" he asks, and I gulp down my nerves.

"Actually, I came to see you," I explain.

He stands in the open doorway as his eyebrows rise. He remains quiet.

"I, uh, brought lunch," I say as I lift the bag. "A peace offering of sorts." I laugh under my breath realizing how ridiculous I must sound.

He lowers his head to run his hand through his hair and by the time he looks back up at me his smile is wide, and his eyes are bright. His shirt is another black button up, but this one has a pink flower print covering the shirt. The top few buttons are left undone leaving a tattoo on his chest to peak through the opening. I've never seen a man look so incredible in a floral print. I've actually never seen a man look so incredible, ever.

"You didn't have to do that." He smiles, his voice is low.

"I know. I wanted to." I shrug.

He moves the door making the opening wider and motions his arm towards the inside of the bookstore. I smile and walk past Samuel as I step inside.

Chapter Thirteen

"So, what's for lunch?" he asks as he follows me inside.

"Oh, I, uh, just stopped at the diner and grabbed a few things." I shrug. I look around and realize there not really a spot to eat. I look over at him and watch him place his hands into his jean pockets.

"I don't really have a spot down here to eat beside a table in the stock room, but it's pretty rough back there." He laughs. "And I put the table away already." He smiles as he sees me look towards the area where we had dinner just last night, even though that night feels like it was weeks ago.

"Oh, I mean that's okay." My cheeks flush. "I'll just leave it here and be on my way." Yup, this was a stupid idea. I place the food on the counter and turn to leave.

"Payton, wait," He stops me and lets out a small laugh. "I just mean, there's nowhere down here. If you don't mind going upstairs, there's a table up there."

"Upstairs?" I ask, I didn't even realize there was an upstairs.

He smiles and begins to walk towards the back of the bookstore, and I follow with the food. We pass through shelf after shelf. There has to be thousands of books here.

Once we get to the very back of the store, I notice a set of metal spiral stairs that take you up to another floor. I follow Samuel up the stairs one by one running my hand over the cold railing. We get to the top and I look around. My eyes are wide as I take in the large studio apartment in front of me.

The furthest wall is exposed brick, just like in my apartment. Except this space is much larger. A small grey couch sits against the brick with a black coffee table in front of it. Next to that is a wall full of windows that offer the most amazing view of the city that surrounds the small bookstore. The floor is hardwood and covered in small rugs that are scattered throughout the space. I see an old record player off in the corner next to the couch. Next to that is a black leather chest on the floor filled with vinyl records. The apartment opens up as I scan to the right and see a small glass dining table with four chairs followed by a small open kitchen with a stainless-steel island separating the space. This place is incredible. Then it hits me, he actually *does* live here. I begin to laugh.

He smiles.

"What's so funny?" he says as he turns towards me.

"I once thought that you spent enough time here to live here, but I didn't think you *actually* lived here." I smile at him and walk over to the glass table, leaving my shoes at the door. I place our lunch on the table.

He laughs. "Well let's just say, owning a bookstore in the twenty-first century doesn't exactly bring in the big bucks. So, I settled here." He walks over to the kitchen and pulls out two plates and two glasses from a cupboard. He pulls open a drawer and grabs silverware as well.

He walks over and sets the table.

"What would you like to drink?" he asks as he looks over at me.

"What do you have?" I ask, taking the lunch containers out of the bag and placing them on the table.

His face flushes.

"Um, water." And we both laugh.

"Water sounds great, actually." I smile and use the silverware to place his burger on his plate. Then I dump my salad on the other plate and drizzle some Caesar dressing over my food.

I go to pull out my chair when I notice he's beat me to it. He's standing behind me waiting for me to take my seat, and I oblige. He joins me at the table in the seat next to me.

He sits down and we spend a few moments in silence. I take a couple bites of my salad and he a few bites of his burger. Then I remember why I'm here and my appetite is lost.

"Um, Samuel…" I pause. "I'm really sorry about this morning." I place my hands in my lap as I watch myself pick at my fingers. He sets his burger down and I feel him watching me.

"I'm a bit of a mess," I laugh, keeping it light. "And I didn't mean to take my lack of sleep out on you." I look up at him and he's wearing a half-smile.

"It's okay, Payton," He says it as if I should already know. "I crossed a line, and I'm sorry," he explains. I offer a similar half-smile.

"It's not that I don't want to share things with you," I continue. "It's just, there are somethings I'm not ready to share yet." I pause, scanning his face, trying to read his thoughts.

He smiles and reaches his hand to mine from under the table. "I understand." He squeezes my hand gently. "And I look forward to the day you are." He offers a sympathetic smile. I cannot believe the terrible things I thought about him just this morning.

"But Samuel, I don't know if that'll ever happen," I reply.

He shrugs. "Then it doesn't."

Eager to change the subject, I ask, "So, um, how long have you lived here?"

He releases my hand and leans back in his chair.

"Pretty much as soon as my dad passed, so about two years or so now. It was just storage before I turned it into this."

He takes a couple more bites of his food.

"It's amazing. The view is breathtaking," I say as I look out of the wall of windows.

Lunch continues as we pick at our food. He tells me about all the junk he had to go through to clean this place out. He had never done anything like this before, so he relied on YouTube how-to videos to teach him all about plumbing, electrical, and drywalling. He makes a joke that this place could come crashing down any second due to his lack of experience. His laugh makes me laugh, and I begin to relax.

After we have finished eating, he gets up and gathers our plates from the table. I thank him as he walks towards the kitchen and places the dishes in the sink.

He walks up to me with his hands in his pockets and smiles.

"You haven't even seen my favorite room in the apartment."

I gulp.

"Oh, um."

I'm unable to connect my mouth to my brain. He begins to laugh.

"No, not like that." He reads my mind. "Just follow me," he says as he reaches his hand out for mine.

I place my hand in his and he walks me over to a door at the back of the apartment. When he opens it, I see a small red room covered with instruments. There's a guitar, a bass, a keyboard, and a bunch of other instruments that I couldn't name. I look at the walls and see them covered in foam, I'm assuming for soundproofing. I walk in and move over to the guitar. I run my fingers down the strings and he studies me from the door.

"Wow, this is incredible. You can play all of these?" I ask.

"Technically, yes. Now, can I play them all well? That's up for debate." He laughs.

"What's your favorite?" I ask as I turn to him.

He ponders the question for a moment. "Hm, probably guitar. It was the first thing I learned."

"Will you play me something?" I ask and his eyebrows rise.

"Um, yeah. I'd love to." He smiles and walks over to the guitar. He grabs it and lifts it over his head. He grabs a stool for me to sit on and grabs a chair for himself. He looks up at me then back down to the guitar and begins to pick at the strings.

He's playing a slow melody, one that I recognize. It's the song we danced to last night, the song I said I loved. His eyes are closed as he continues. I scan his face. He looks so calm and I can tell he's well practiced by the fluidity of his playing. It doesn't even look like he has to try, it comes so naturally to him. I close my eyes and begin to sway to the music. With my eyes closed, I picture the evening we had last night. Samuel holding me close as we swayed back and forth to this song. The smell of his cologne clinging to my shirt. Seeing the candlelight flicker across his face, lighting up his dark eyes. We were slow dancing in a burning room.

I open my eyes as the melody comes to an end. Samuel looks at me, I hadn't noticed how close I had got to him as he was playing. He leans forward, slightly, his guitar between us. The air is thick. Our eyes meet and my heart rate picks up. He takes his calloused hand and runs his thumb across my bottom lip, quickening my breath. I wait, impatiently, as my chest rises and falls with his.

His hand moves to my cheek as I feel a chill from the rings adorned on his fingers. I lean into his hand, leading him to close our gap. He rests his forehead against mine and locks his eyes to mine.

"Payton," he whispers.

"Samuel," I whisper back. My heart is beating so hard I'm sure he can hear it.

Our words hang between us for just a moment for I can't take it any more, and I take his mouth in mine. I can taste the familiarity of mint on his tongue as he runs it against mine. I stretch my arm across the guitar and place my hands in his hair and gripping softly. He moans into my mouth, delivering the sweetest taste.

He pulls back for just a moment to take the guitar off and places it back on the stand. He pulls me off the stool and onto his lap as he reconnects our lips. He pulls out each hair pin holding my bun together and my hair falls onto my shoulders. He raises his hands and takes a handful of my hair in each, pulling me closer into him. I move both hands to his chest and I dig my fingers into his shirt. I roll my hips into him and I can feel his readiness below me. He moves his hands to my hips and pulls me in, closing any possible gap there could be between us. I hardly know this man, but in this moment, I feel like I've known him forever and if I don't have him right now, I will actually combust.

My body takes over my mind as I bring my hands to the buttons of his shirt and begin to undo them. I only make it down three buttons when he pulls away from me. I watch him scan my face, trying to read my mind as I try to read his.

"Are you sure you want to do this?" he asks, almost too quietly to hear, as he glances at my hands stopped on the fourth button. I look into his dark eyes and watch his chest pump up and down. All I can muster is a nod.

"Well." He pauses. "Not here." He laughs as he looks around the cluttered room full of instruments. He gives me a small kiss as he helps me off his lap. He stands up and takes my hand in his and walks me out of this room and into the room across the hall. His bedroom is much larger than the music room. His bed sits in the center of the main wall with a large black dresser against the wall across from the bed. I notice a few shirts scattered across the floor as I look around. I notice him watch me as he runs his hand through his hair.

"Sorry." He laughs softy. "I wasn't really expecting company." His face flushes as he looks around his room.

I turn towards him and place my hands in his.

"It's perfect," I reply.

He laughs. "You are a terrible liar." He pulls me into him, and we begin to pick up where we left off in the music room. I undo the rest of his buttons, faster and more frantically than I'd like to admit and his shirt drops to the floor. I run my hands up his tattooed arms and onto his chest. His muscles are tone, and I can feel each one move under my touch. I feel his hands at the bottom of my shirt as he pulls it over my head, exposing my plain black bra. I really wish I would have changed. He wraps his hands around my hips and digs his fingers into my skin. My hands fumble to remove his heavy black leather belt as I slip it out of each belt loop. He begins to nip down my neck.

He walks into me and gently guides me towards the large bed and lifts me on top of the mattress. He wraps an arm around my waist and lifts me further onto the bed like I weight nothing, all while keeping his lips on mine. His arms are on each side of me holding himself above me. I run my hands down his hard stomach until I reach his jeans, and I begin to undo the button first, then the zipper. He pulls away from me and stands at the edge of the bed. He brings his jeans down to his ankles and steps out of them. His black boxer-briefs are growing tighter as he crawls back onto the bed and begins to remove my jeans. He pulls them down gently as he leaves a kiss every inch down my stomach and onto my thigh as he tosses my jeans on the floor.

He holds himself over me as his hair tickles the top of my forehead. He takes his knee and separates my legs as he gently pushes himself against me. I arch my back, as the friction alone is almost enough to send me over the edge. He moves his hands down between my legs and cups my center. I feel him smile when he feels that I am ready for him.

"Payton?" he whispers in my ear. "You're perfect." The hair on the back of my neck raises with the unexpected praise.

He takes my underwear in each hand and slides them down my legs. He props himself on his elbow next to me and begins to once again trace my tongue with his. His other hand gently glides down my body, until I feel his finger enter me. I moan into his mouth, making him kiss me harder. Then a second finger joins the first. I can feel his cold rings as he moves.. I wrap my hand into his hair and tug gently, inciting a moan from him. His thumb circles over the bundle of nerves that he has pulsating. He pulls his fingers back and forth until I'm nearly there. I tighten my legs when he pauses, attempting to offer myself relief, and I feel him smile.

"Not yet," he whispers as he removes his fingers from me and tugs his briefs down. He leans over to his nightstand and pulls out a foil packet from the drawer. He uses his teeth to rip open the packet and removes the condom. He goes to place it on himself when I pause him, taking the condom from his hands. He watches me as I place it over him and roll it down. He groans in my ear and sends goosebumps down my neck. He uses his knee to separate my legs further and enters me. I gasp as I dig my fingers into his back. I grip so hard I wouldn't be surprised if I drew blood, but he doesn't seem to mind either way. He moves back and forth at a painstakingly slow pace. Teasing every ounce of self-control I have. As he moves, he takes his thumb and rubs it over those nerves causing the pit in my stomach to build. I begin to grip tighter into his hair as his tongue explores my entire mouth.

"Samuel, please," I beg. He pulls back and looks at me before slamming his hips into me and quickening his pace, offering me relief. I throw my head back and feel every part of him.

The build keeps going and I'm nearly there when he whispers, "Just let go." It's those words that send me over the edge. I arch my back as he moans into my neck finishing right behind me.

He stays above me for a few moments as he sighs into my neck, his head buried in my hair. After he catches his breath, he plants small kisses along my neck and up to my jawline. He pulls back and studies my face. He takes his hand and tucks my wild hair behind my ear as he tugs at my earlobe.

"I'm really glad you came by today," he says, almost at a whisper.

I smile. "Me too."

At this point I've become increasingly aware that I am naked in his apartment while a business is being run right underneath our feet.

"We, uh, better get dressed." I laugh and he helps me off the bed. I watch him tie off the condom and toss it in the trash next to his bed. I become insecure at the thought of how many other women have been here. He says he hasn't been on a date since Allison, but that doesn't mean he hasn't brought women back for... not-dates. Clearly, all it takes is for him to play his guitar and women probably throw themselves at him. My face flushes as I realize I am now in that category.

"What?" he says with a smile as he buttons his jeans.

"Um, nothing. I just can't find my shirt," I say as I step into my jeans.

He walks over to a chair in the corner where the shirt was hanging. I nod as I grab it from him and pull it over my head.

"Nice shirt, by the way," he says as he begins to button his.

"Oh, thanks." I shrug as I watch his tattoos move on top of his muscles as he finishes buttoning his shirt. My face flushes when I notice him notice me staring at every inch of him.

"Oh, and you never told me you had tattoos." he smiles teasingly at me as I roll my eyes and pin my hair back up into a bun. I gently nudge him as I walk out of the room, Samuel following behind me.

Chapter Fourteen

I walk towards the door and begin to put on my shoes.

"Oh, um, you're leaving?" Samuel asks and I turn to him.

"I guess I was just trying not to overstay my welcome." I laugh nervously. He walks over to me. He's left the top half of his shirt unbuttoned and I can't help but scan his chest.

"I doubt you could do that," he laughs. "I mean, if you want to leave, that's totally fine. But don't leave because you think I want you to. Because I don't." He offers a small smile as he runs his hand through his now very messy hair.

I glance at the clock, it's only three p.m. and it's not like I have any other plans this evening. Even if I did, I'd definitely miss them for him.

"You don't have to go back downstairs?" I ask.

"No, Sarah's got it handled. I'm just gonna go let her know that I'll be busy today," he answers. "Just give me a minute," he adds as he kisses my forehead and walks down the metal staircase. I could get used to this.

He returns just moments later and walks into the apartment. I'm standing over by the window when I feel him walk up behind me. I turn towards him.

"Well," he shrugs. "You've got me for the whole day." He smiles. "Anything you'd like to do?"

"Hm," I put my finger to my chin pretending I'm deep in thought, "How about... ice cream?" I smile.

He laughs, "Ice cream? Yeah, I guess I could go for some ice cream." He grabs my hand and pulls me towards him. He wraps his arms around my shoulders, and I wrap mine around his waist. He looks down at me and smiles. He plants a small kiss on my forehead then leans down and kisses my lips.

We walk down the spiral stairs together with my hand is his. Once we reach the bottom my cheeks flush as I look up and see Sarah carrying a box full of books.

"Oh, so this is the very important business meeting you have that's taking you away all day?" she says, teasing her brother.

"Most definitely. Very important stuff," he teases back as he nudges my arm.

"Well, try not to get into too much trouble." She winks as she walks towards the front of the store.

With my hand still in his he walks me out of the back door of the bookstore. It takes us into a small alleyway. He leads me to the left until we walk into another cobblestone street full of shops. I don't think I've been down this one yet.

"Are you sure it's okay to leave Sarah to man the bookstore all by herself?" I feel bad for 'stealing' Samuel away.

He laughs. "Yes. We probably get fewer than thirty customers a day, and the day is already almost over. There's not much to it." He gently squeezes my hand in his.

"There's an ice cream place, there," he says as he points across the street. I nod and allow him to lead the way.

We walk up to the window and I order a small chocolate cone with sprinkles. He orders a vanilla milkshake. We take our orders and find a small round table to sit at.

"Vanilla milkshake, huh?" I ask.

"Yeah, what's wrong with that?" He smiles as he takes a sip.

"Just a little boring." I tease him.

"Oh, you think so? Well, there's nothing wrong with a little vanilla," he winks as he nudges my arm and I blush, "Plus, you just ordered the world's smallest chocolate cone with regular... what did you call them? Sprinkles?" He laughs.

"Hey, sprinkles are amazing, okay?" I laugh as I take a bite of my ice cream.

"So, is that where you get it then?" he asks. I pause and smile, unsure of how to answer.

"There's no way you were born this amazing," he continues. "That's just not possible." He takes a sip from his shake.

I roll my eyes at him and continue eating my ice cream.

"So…" I take a deep breath. "Um, how often does that happen?" I can't believe I'm asking him this.

"How often does what happen?" he asks, unsure of where I'm going with this.

"Ya know, hot guy plays guitar, girl throws herself at him. It's pretty clichéd." I smile as my cheeks flush as I attempt to make a joke at my own expense.

He laughs, a big laugh.

"Are you asking me if I sleep with a lot of girls?" He teases me.

I roll my eyes and bump my shoulder into his.

"Or did you just want an excuse to call me hot?" He raises one eyebrow as he smiles.

"Samuel!" I beg, as I'm now really embarrassed by my question.

"Okay, okay," he replies. "Well, to answer your very invasive question," — my cheeks flush even more — "I already told you, I haven't dated since Allison."

"I know but dating someone and sleeping with someone aren't the same," I reply.

"Yeah, true, I guess. But no, I haven't been with anyone, in that way, or any way. Not since her." He fidgets with his straw. "So wait a minute, are we dating? Or are you just sleeping with me?" he asks as he pretends to be offended.

I pop the last bite of ice cream cone into my mouth and give him a sarcastic shrug.

"Ugh, you women are all the same." He smiles as he teases me. I begin to laugh with him.

We finish our desserts and sit in silence for just a moment.

"So, um, my band is playing at the pub tonight." He starts spinning his rings around his fingers. He's nervous.

"Oh?" I reply.

"I'd really love for you to come. You could bring your friend, from the coffee house, and his girlfriend." He studies my face trying to guess my reply.

I think about how I do have to work tomorrow, but my shift doesn't start until noon, and I wouldn't mind meeting up with Noah and Olivia. They are my only friends here, well, besides Samuel now.

"Yeah, sure." I shake my head yes and his eyes light up.

"Okay, awesome." He lets out a sigh of relief.

We get up from the table and walk down the cobblestone street. He grabs my hand and holds it in his as we weave though the crowded street. We stop into a few shops here and there, but Samuel never lets my hand leave his for more than a moment. As we stroll, he occasionally brings the back of my hand up to his lips and plants small kisses across my knuckles. I begin to notice how people look at him as we walk. I get it, from the outside he looks a little intimidating. Okay, very intimidating. But they don't know the Samuel that I know, the kind sweet person that I know. I don't care about his dark past because that's just what it is, the past. I may not have known him back then, but I know he's different now. I think he's different now. Well, I hope.

Chapter Fifteen

On the way back to Samuel's apartment I text Noah.

ME: Hey! Live music at the pub tn?

NOAH: Sure! We'll be there!

As we get back to the bookstore, Samuel's and I take the stairs back up into his apartment. By the time we get back it's around six thirty p.m. Samuel says his band is supposed to go on at eight p.m..

He walks over to the kitchen and grabs us two glasses of water. I go over to the small grey couch and sit on one side, close to the windows. He walks over to the couch with two waters in hand and places them on the table. He rummages through the black case full of records and pulls one out. He places it on the record player and a soft indie ballad fills the apartment. He sits on the other side and lays his arm across the back of the couch.

"Come here," he says quietly and motions his hand, calling me over. I smile and move to the other side of the couch and lean into him, his arm wrapping around me. He places a small kiss on the top of my head as I melt into him. We sit like this while the first song plays. As the next song starts, he clears his throat.

"I have a question," he states.

"Um, yes?" I ask nervously.

"What's your greatest fear?" he asks softly, playing with my fingers between his.

I ponder the question for a moment, wondering how open I'm willing to be. After a few moments I reply, "Being found."

He let out a quiet laugh, "Um, care to elaborate on that?" I feel him looking at me.

"No," I laugh as I lay my head back on his chest, "Your turn. Your biggest fear?" I ask.

He's silent for a moment before he answers, "Losing the one I love most." I feel the heaviness in his answer, and I think of Allison.

"Care to elaborate?" I repeat his question to him.

He laughs, "I don't think I need to."

We sit like this for a while, our bodies sitting together, him playing with my hands as we intertwine them together. I run my finger across each black nail and spin each ring around his finger. He takes a thick silver ring off his of his smallest finger and slides it over my ring finger. It's huge, and I laugh. He takes it off my ring finger and places it over my thumb. It fits perfectly. I stare at it for a few seconds.

"Keep it," he says into my hair, almost in a whisper. I turn and face him.

"Are you sure?" I ask, I know better than to protest much more than that. He nods his head and places his hand on my cheek. He leans in and presses his lips to mine. I feel my stomach start to flutter. His tongue parts my lips and it traces against mine. I pull myself on top of his lap and he grabs my waist, pulling me closer to him. I take both of my hands and bury them in his hair, gently pulling his head back to deepen the kiss.

"We have to leave soon," I say breathlessly into the kiss. He groans. I can feel him growing beneath me.

"I know," he growls. I reluctantly pull away from the kiss. There's a pause between us.

"So, giving me your ring…" I begin, breaking the silence.

He laughs, "Yeah, and?" He tucks some hair behind my ear.

"Does that mean I'm…" I pause, embarrassed to finish my sentence.

"My girlfriend?" He finishes it for me as his eyebrows rise. My face flushes and I feel juvenile.

"Sorry, I don't want you to think that you have to call me that just because of today." I shift uncomfortably, still in his lap.

"I'd want nothing more," he says as he studies my face. I smile as I spin his ring around my thumb. He grabs my hand and kisses each finger, ending with my thumb.

I glance at the clock behind us, it's already quarter to eight.

"Oh my God, we have to go," I say as I crawl off his lap. I grab his hands and pull him off the couch.

He groans.

"Fine. Let me grab my things." He disappears into his music room and returns with his guitar in a case.

"Ready?" he asks and I nod. I follow him down the stairs and walk towards the front of the bookstore. We both wave goodbye to Sarah as she looks to have finished closing up the store. She waves goodbye as we walk outside.

We walk into the pub and I scan the room for Noah and Olivia. I see them in the center of the bar and squeeze Samuel's hand before separating from him to walk over to their table. Samuel walks over to the stage.

"Um, did I just see you walk in with that guy?" Olivia practically screams.

I turn to look at Samuel on the stage. He sees me and smiles as he prepares for his set. I turn back to my table.

"Um, yeah." I smile.

"They were together this morning too." Noah playfully bumps his shoulder to mine. I roll my eyes.

"Oh my God! Spill!" Olivia says in an attempt to elicit some sort of 'girl talk' from me.

I go to speak but Samuel's voice comes across the microphone. I mouth 'sorry' to Olivia and turn to watch the stage. It's pretty impossible to have a conversation with the band playing.

"Good evening everyone," Samuel announces; everyone in the bar cheers. "We're Bridge I Burn, and I hope you enjoy the set we have for you tonight." He looks over at me and winks.

I'm nodding my head along to the first song. I watch Samuel as he plays his guitar and sings a folk-sounding rhythm into the mic, a much different sound than the first night I heard him. Clearly, he has a wide range of music he enjoys playing. He sings with his eyes closed as his hair falls over his forehead. It sticks to his skin as his forehead begins to collect sweat. My stomach flutters at the thought of that exact guitar in his apartment and what it led to. My cheeks flush even though no one else can hear my thoughts. Those thoughts are interrupted by a waitress walking up to me, wine in hand.

"Oh, I didn't order this," I say, thinking it's a mistake.

"I know, he did. For you," she says as she gestures towards Samuel. I smile at her and nod, taking the glass.

The next four songs he plays don't last nearly long enough. I love watching him play, he looks so happy and content.

"Thank you everyone! We're Bridges I Burn, and I hope you had a fantastic night." Samuel signs off with the crowd. I turn back towards my table and take the last sip from my wine glass.

"So?" Olivia says, clearly not forgetting that she wants details. I start to speak when I feel a hand on the small of my back. I turn, already knowing who it is, and I see Samuel.

"How was it? Crock of shit, huh?" He smiles.

"No, it was amazing. You guys were great." I smile. I notice Olivia moving her eyes back and forth between me and Samuel.

"Um, Samuel, you met Noah," I nod towards Noah and Noah lifts his hand to a wave and nods back with a smile. "And this is his girlfriend, Olivia. Olivia, this is

Samuel, my, uh, boyfriend." The words feel foreign on my tongue. Olivia's eyes light up.

"Boyfriend?" she practically screams. My face flushes. She reaches across the table to shake his hand. "Hello, boyfriend Samuel." He laughs as he runs his fingers through his hair with one hand and shakes hers with the other.

"You can call me Sam," he yells over the table. The bar crowd is getting loud, making it hard to hear. I check the time on my phone and it's almost eleven p.m. I lean into Samuel.

"I better go, I have work tomorrow." I feel like I'm yelling into his ear.

"I'll come with you," he replies. I look over at the table full of bandmates as they yell Samuel's name to join them.

"No, you don't have to. You should stay with them." I gesture over to his friends.

"At least let me walk you home. It's become a bit of a tradition." He laughs. I agree to let him walk me home and I say my goodbyes to Noah and Olivia.

Samuel and I leave the pub and begin to walk down the street. Samuel takes his leather jacket and drapes it over my shoulders.

"So, you introduced me as your boyfriend," he says with a smile. My face flushes.

"Oh, I mean, I just thought after our conversation today," I stammer, "that... that was okay." He laughs and runs his hand through his hair.

"Of course it's okay. I just really loved hearing you say it." He smiles and looks down at the concrete. We walk in a comfortable silence for most of the way to my apartment. Samuel holds my hand almost the entire way. We arrive at my door and I turn to him and remove his jacket. He reluctantly takes his jacket and wraps it around himself.

"Thank you for coming," he says as he places his hand on my cheek.

"Of course." I look up at him. He leans down and kisses my lips. After we part, I look at him, pulling my bottom lip between my teeth, rocking back and forth on my feet. He laughs.

"What?" he asks.

"Um, would you like to come in?" I ask. His eyes widen along with his smile. "Unless, you want to get back to your friends. Which is totally fine if you—" He cuts me off with a kiss.

After a moment he pulls away.

"I'd love to," he whispers.

Chapter Sixteen

I open the door into my apartment, scrambling to find the light switch. Once I do the apartment lights a dim glow.

"It's not much." I shrug. "But it's home." I remove my shoes and hang my bag up on the hook next to the door.

"It's a really nice place. Really," Samuel says as he hangs his leather jacket next to my bag. I grab his hand and slowly lead him upstairs, skipping a tour.

We walk into my bedroom and I drop his hand at the top of the stairs.

"This is where the magic doesn't happen." I laugh at my own terrible joke. What am I on? *MTV Cribs*?

He laughs with me. "Where the magic doesn't happen?" I nod and cover my mouth as I laugh. He walks up to me and gently pulls my hand down off my face.

"Don't ever cover up your smile, please. It's beautiful," he whispers, holding both of my hands in his. I only had one glass of wine, but I skipped dinner, so my brain is feeling a little fuzzy.

I remove my hands from his and bring my hands to his chest. I begin to unbutton his shirt for the second time today. He takes in a sharp breath.

"You're insatiable," he whispers.

"Have you seen you?"

We laugh softly together.

"Have *you* seen *you*?" he returns as he looks me in the eyes, but it feels like he's looking into me.

Once I undo every button, I slide the shirt off his shoulders and allow it to drop to the floor. I run my hands over his sculpted chest and watch goosebumps take over his skin. He gently grabs my wrist, making me wince. He pauses and looks at me, somehow letting me know that it's okay. That he's not going to hurt me. He begins to plant small kisses across my palm, up my wrist, and finishes at the pit of my elbow.

He grabs the bottom of my shirt and begins to lift it off. Of course, it gets stuck in my hair pins. I laugh as I untangle myself and toss my shirt on the floor. I reach up and grab the pins out of my hair, allowing my hair to fall. He moves my hair behind my shoulder and traces the outline of my collar bone with his fingers, returning the goosebumps. He takes his hand and traces it up my back and meets the back of my bra. He pops open the clasp with one hand. I let the straps fall down my shoulder allowing it to fall. He runs his hand along the bottom of my breast, his thumb flicking across the center. I start to feel a pulse in between my legs. He leans down and kisses me down my neck and across my collar bone.

Just barely keeping it together, my hands find his jeans and I unbutton them, sliding them down his legs, as he steps out of them. His briefs growing tighter and tighter. He walks towards me, leading me to the bed. The back of

114

my knees meet my bed and I crawl backwards onto the mattress as Samuel follows me. My head finds a pillow and I pull Samuel closer to me. Our lips meet and his tongue instantly separates mine. I run my fingers up his back and dig them into his skin. He moans and he pushes deeper into my mouth. I hear him moan my name and I feel an electric current surge through my body. I can taste his want with every gasped breath.

He pulls away from me.

"I want to taste you, all of you," he says breathlessly. I nod giving him permission to do absolutely anything he wants. He plants small kisses down my stomach and pulls my jeans down, my underwear going with. My thighs tense as I think about what's coming next.

"Relax baby," he says as he pushes my thighs further apart. He places one finger inside of me and my back arches. He wraps his other hand around my thigh, keeping it still. As he pulls his finger out, he adds a second and he goes back in. He tightens his grip and I wither underneath him. He kisses the inside of my thigh until his tongue meets the nerves at the center of my body. He gently sucks and he moves his fingers in and out. I gasp for breath.

"Are you okay?" he asks as he looks up. I nod as I reach my hand down to his hair and grip it in my hand. He smiles and begins again. He teases my center with his tongue, sending shock waves through my body, fingers moving in and out. I don't know how much more I can take. I begin to feel the pit in my gut start to build.

"I want you to come like this," he says in between sucks. That statement gives me what I need to come completely undone by his touch. My head goes back, and my jaw drops open moaning out his name. As I relax, he looks up at me and places both of his fingers into his mouth.

"Incredible, baby." He groans. He moves back up and begins to move his briefs down.

"You taste so good," he says as he kisses along my jawline. He stretches off the bed and grasps at his pants. He rummages through the pockets and pulls out the foil packet. He rips it with his teeth and spits the ripped piece onto the floor. He goes to put it on then pauses. He moves back over to me and holds the condom up to me.

"Would you like to do the honors?" he asks with a smile. I smile back and nod as I take the condom and roll it over him as I feel him pulse. He groans as I rub my thumb over the tip. I sit up and rotate his shoulders until I am on top of him, his back leaning against the headboard. I slowly sit down onto him, feeling every inch fill inside of me. He groans as he digs his fingers into my hips and guides me down. I begin to rock while simultaneously pumping him in and out of me. I feel him continue to grow, tightening inside. My hands grip his chest and I watch the muscle beneath his skin tighten with each pulse. I tighten the muscles of my center around him, creating an even tighter pull between us.

"Fuck!" he groans as I watch every muscles on his body tighten, his fingers digging into my hips. I feel him pulse as he finishes. He drops his head against the headboard and attempts to catch his breath.

I lean down and kiss along his jawline and down his neck. I pull myself off him and lay my head on his shoulder. He pulls the condom off and ties it closed. He finds the garbage bin next to my bed and tosses it in. He pulls back the covers and pulls them over us. I rest my head on his chest and listen to the sound of his heartbeat. He grabs my hands with his and intertwines our fingers. He kisses the pad on each finger and stop at my thumb that has his ring on it. He rolls the ring between his fingers and I can feel him smiling.

"You really are amazing, you know that?" he whispers. I smile as I tap my fingers across his chest. He pulls me in and kisses the top of my forehead.

He sighs. "Goodnight, Payton."

"Goodnight, Samuel," I reply.

Chapter Seventeen

He's on top of me. Breathing the smell of cheap liquor into my face. It's nauseating. I struggle underneath him, but he has both of my hands gripped tightly in his one large hand. He hits them against the headboard, our wedding bands clinking against the wood. He uses the other to yank down my shorts. The more I fight, the tighter his grip becomes. I feel my fingers start to go numb. The tears falling down my face come to a stop and my fight is dwindling. This feeling is all too familiar, and I know exactly what's going to happen.

"I'd do anything for you," he growls as he takes off his belt with one hand and pulls his jeans down to his knees. He moves his hand to my throat and uses all of his weight to push down, keeping me still. I feel the forcefulness of him as he tears me in two. My hands are still wrestling in his grip. The room starts to blur as the pressure on my throat becomes heavier. I try to gasp for breath, but I can't. I try to kick my legs beneath him, but my entire body feels numb. I can't breathe. I can't...

I wake up gasping for air. I shoot up in bed and grab my neck. I still feel the heaviness pressing down on my throat. I begin to cough, like I've been holding my breath for an hour. I'm panting, trying to get as much air into my lungs as possible. I feel a hand touch my arm and I rip myself away, jumping out of bed and backing myself against the wall next to the bed. My vision is blurry.

As my surroundings come into focus, I see Samuel sitting up in bed with a terrified expression on his face. As my breathing becomes more controlled, I notice my hands are still grasping my neck. Samuel looks at me, horrified, like he's trying to read my thoughts.

I drop my hands and walk over to the stairs. I grab Samuel's shirt off the ground and wrap it around me as I walk downstairs. I pull the collar to my nose and breath in his cologne, calming my knotted stomach. I walk into the kitchen, grab a glass out of the cupboard, and fill it with water. I gulp down half the glass in one sip. I place the glass in the sink and turn around. I jump at the dark figure at the bottom of the stairs. But it only takes a second before I realize who it is.

"Payton?" Samuel whispers and he walks over to the kitchen. I lean my hands against the countertop facing him. He walks over and runs his hand down my arm. I flinch at the touch and he pulls his hand away.

"Um, I'm sorry I woke you," I say into the countertop, my head hanging and my voice hoarse. He cautiously places his hands on my shoulders, pausing, waiting for another flinch, but in contrast, I relax. He pulls me into him and moves my head to his chest. I begin to feel tears fall.

I'm quietly sobbing into his chest as he holds me in the dark. The only light we have is from a streetlamp just outside as it shines through the window. He runs his hand through my hair and gently strokes the back of my head. We remain like this for what feels like hours.

My sobs disappear and my tears dry against his chest. He pulls me back and studies my face before he speaks.

He sighs. "Payton," he says as he tucks a loose piece of hair behind my ear. "I... I will never let anything bad happen to you." His dark eyes looking deep into mine. "So as long as I'm here, you're safe. Please know that."

I can tell he means it, as much as he can. He kisses the center of my forehead and my eyes close at his touch. I nod and grab his hand, leading us back upstairs. We crawl back into bed, no words or questions between us, and this I am thankful for. He lies on his back and opens his arm, inviting me to his chest. He pulls me in, and I stretch my arm over his torso, mimicking his pull. I run my fingers over his abdomen, following the lines of his tattoos, until I drift off to sleep.

I wake up to the golden glow of the sunrise piercing through the bedroom window. I look over and Samuel is still deep in sleep. I grab my phone and check the time, six a.m.. I slowly roll off the bed, careful not to wake him. He stirs lightly but remains asleep. I quietly grab my running clothes from the dresser at the foot of the bed and walk into the bathroom. I shut the door and walk over to the sink. I splash cold water on my face and wash away the tear stains on my cheeks. My hair goes up in a high bun and I slip my leggings on first. I run my hands down Samuel's shirt which I'm still wearing. I slowly unbutton it as I wish I could live in this shirt. I bring my sports bra down over my head and walk back into the bedroom. I lay his shirt across the chair by my closet. I find a scrap of paper and a pen and write a note for Samuel.

Be back soon - P

I place it on the table next to the bed and walk down the stairs, careful to avoid as many creaks as I can. I put my headphones in and step outside. The weather is a bit chilly, but the sunrise is beautiful. I start pounding my feet to the pavement, breathing in as much fresh air as I can.

Today I decide to run past the coffee shop. Samuel is back at my apartment and I'd like to spend as much of the morning with him as I can before I go into work. I arrive back at my apartment and open the door. I smell the incredible smell of freshly brewed coffee and… pastries? I remove my headphones and walk over to the kitchen. Samuel is pouring a fresh cup of coffee and has a large brown paper bag sitting on the counter. His hair is perfectly messy, and he's dressed, but he's left his shirt unbuttoned. He looks incredible.

"Good morning," he smiles, and turns to the fridge to find the creamer.

"Top shelf," I smile, and I watch him scan the fridge.

"Ah," he says, as he grabs it and pours a small amount into the coffee cup.

I approach the counter and he slides the cup over to me. I take a sip as I eye the large bag.

"Oh, I ran to the bakery and picked up some breakfast." He shrugs. "I didn't know what you'd want, so

I went a little overboard and grabbed a bit of everything." He laughs.

"Thank you," I reply softly, and I rummage through the bag. I find a blueberry scone and hear Noah in my head say, 'The usual?' I laugh to myself and pull it out of the bag.

"Yeah, I figured that was a safe bet." He laughs, in on the joke, as he pours himself a cup of coffee. He takes it black. I take a few bites of the scone, alternating with hot sips of coffee. The warm coffee unties the knot in my stomach.

After a few moments of silence, I look up at Samuel, "I'm sorry I left you alone this morning, I just needed to clear my head." I offer a smile.

"I know." He smiles. "You've mentioned that you tend to go for a run when you have…" he pauses and scans my face, unsure if he should continue. I nod, releasing him from having to finish.

I motion my head towards the couch, silently inviting him with me. He smiles and searches through the bag, pulling out a blueberry muffin. We walk over to the couch, coffee and pastries in hand.

He sits longways on the couch, stretching his legs out in front of him, leaving a gap in the middle of his legs for me. I oblige and sit between his knees and lay back onto his chest. We sit like this in comfortable silence as we enjoy our breakfast. I look out the window and watch as the light from the golden sunrise slowly covers each building. Samuel begins to rub my shoulders. My muscles relax as I melt into his touch. I lay my head back and look up at him. He looks down at my face and places his hand on my cheek. He pulls me in for a kiss and holds it. This is where I feel the safest.

Chapter Eighteen

The sun is almost completely up, and I need to shower. I'm pretty sure I just caught a whiff of myself, and it's rough.

"I need to shower, like now," I laugh, and I stand up from the couch. I begin to walk over to the stairs, and I hear Samuel stand.

"Mind if I uh…" he runs his hands through his hair. I nod, answering his question before he finishes. He smiles and follows me upstairs.

I've never been one to shower with someone else. It always felt cramped and I could always finish what I needed to do ten times faster when I was in the shower alone. But something about Samuel makes me want to experience every piece of our day together. I warn him that we have about fifteen minutes of warm water before it gets cold. He begins to undress. He slides his already unbuttoned shirt off and tosses it on the floor. He undoes his thick black belt and pulls it out of each belt loop. His tattoos are rolling over his muscles, across his chest and down his arm. His tattoos are mostly small, but there's a lot. He undoes his jeans and slides them down along with his briefs, stepping out of them as they wrinkle on the floor. I can tell I'm staring, but I can't pull my eyes away. He notices as he laughs to himself and walks over to me.

"Need help?' he asks with a playful smile. I laugh and nod, lifting my arms above my head. He grabs my sports bra and wrestles the tight material over my head, tossing it by his shirt on the floor. He pulls my hair tie out, dropping my hair to my back. His hands meet my waistband and he gently tugs.

"Jesus," he says as he tugs harder. "Are these things glued to you?" He laughs as he tugs even harder, finally freeing the fabric from my legs. I lean into the shower and turn the knob. It takes a moment for the water to warm, and when it does, I step inside and hold the shower door open, inviting him in.

He steps behind me, I'm facing the shower head allowing the water to hit my chest. He runs his hands over my shoulders and across my neck. I take in a sharp breath. He leans down and grabs the soap and squeezes it into his hands. He rubs his hands together and begins to massage my body. He starts at my shoulders, kneading his fingers, then makes his way down my arms, gently squeezing as he goes. His hands reach around to my stomach, takes one finger and softly traces up my torso and stops at my breasts. He takes both hands and gently caresses them, running his thumbs over the center. I lay my head back on his shoulder and try to control my breathing.

"Relax baby," he whispers as he wraps one arm across my chest, holding me still. His other hand, still soapy, runs back down the center of my abdomen and greets the nerves in the center of my body. He rolls the bud in between his thumb and his index finger. I take a sharp breath in, trying to follow his instruction. I feel him growing into my back as he gently presses into me. He continues to circle his fingers around and I feel the build. My pit is growing until it feels like it's in my throat. Just as I almost reach the top, I feel him slip his finger into me. I become completely undone by that touch, my knees becoming weak. Samuel tightens his grip around my chest, holding me up as I try to come back down to earth.

Once I get feeling back in my legs, I turn to him and study him. I reach down slowly and grab his length in my hands. I run my thumb over the tip and feel him twitch at my touch. He runs his fingers through his wet hair and parts his mouth, waiting for my next move. I begin to bend my knees to return the favor when the water turns ice-cold.

"Oh, fuck!" Samuel yells.

I jump up and goosebumps cover my body. We both start laughing as we grab the shampoo and quickly try to wash our hair in the freezing cold water.

I jump out as soon as I rinse the conditioner from my hair and Samuel follows me.

"That was not fifteen minutes!" He laughs as he grabs a towel and runs it over his hair.

"I'd call fifteen minutes the average." I laugh as I wrap a towel around myself. I grab my phone and check the time, it's almost nine a.m. Samuel dries off and begin to get dressed as I blow-dry my hair. I watch him from the mirror. Even watching him put clothes back on is incredibly attractive. I finish blow-drying my hair and I walk into the bedroom. Samuel is sitting on the edge of the bed scrolling through his phone, waiting for me. I walk up to him and he looks up at me.

"So, you have some time to kill before work, right?" he asks. "What do you want to do?" He sets his phone on the table next to the bed, next to my note. I smile at him as my knees reach the floor in front of him. His eyes go dark and the corners of his mouth curl up.

"Oh," he says as he pulls off the towel I have wrapped around me, dropping it to the floor. I undo his belt just at the front and unbutton his jeans. He lifts his hips as I pull his jeans down to his ankles. His briefs follow. I take him in my hand and begin to stroke, feeling him grow. He leans back on his elbows while looking at me. I tease him a bit more by running my thumb over the tip. He rolls his eyes back as I take him into my mouth. I take him in as far as I can, using my grip to compensate for the rest. He groans as I take him in and out.

"Baby," he groans, "I'm going to finish soon, so if you don't…" He tries to catch his breath. I pump harder and faster. "Fuck, if you don't want it in your mouth, I need you to stop." I tighten the grip on my hands and run my tongue across the tip. He reaches down and takes a handful of my hair as he spills into my mouth.

I stand up and rewrap the towel around my body as he lies on the bed, panting. He leans back up on his elbows and looks at me.

127

"You are the sexiest woman alive; did you know that?" he says, still breathless. My face flushes as I roll my eyes and walk over to my closet. He is literally the most attractive man I've ever met, in every way. But hearing him call *me* sexy just seems like a far jump.

Chapter Nineteen

I grab my work clothes out of the closet as I hear Samuel refasten his belt. I get myself dressed in my work uniform and pull my hair into a sleek ponytail. I walk into the bathroom, brush my teeth, and add a small amount of mascara to try and bring my tired eyes to life.

I walk back into the bedroom and Samuel is standing by the stairs, waiting for me.

"Ready?" he asks as he holds his hand out for mine. I nod and place my hand in his and we walk down the stairs together. He gets to the door and shrugs his leather jacket on. I grab my thin black jacket and wrap it around me and drape my bag over my shoulder.

He stops at the door and turns around. He places my face in his hands and locks eyes with me. We hold still for just a moment before he smiles and places a kiss on my forehead.

I've never had this feeling. This feeling of peace and magnetism. Feeling as if my entire world has been disrupted, but in the best way. I'm so completely drawn to him that I feel as if I would lose the very drive to breathe without him.

We walk out the door, and I turn to lock it. Our hands reconnect as we walk in the direction of the bookstore. We walk at a slow pace, enjoying each other's company, trying to spend as much time together as we can before my shift. His thumb rubs over mine and I lean in closer to him. His leather jacket is cold, but also soft and comforting.

We arrive at the bookstore and the sign on the door reads *'Closed'*. Samuel unlocks the door with his bundle of keys and flips the sign to *'Open'* as we walk in. The bell dings as the door closes behind us. The bookstore is dark when Samuel walks behind the counter and flips a bunch of switches, illuminating the entire store.

"I need to change, care to join?" he asks as he points up towards the ceiling. I glance at my phone: it's already eleven a.m.

"Um, sure. I have to leave soon though." The diner is just down the road, about a five-minute walk. But I do like to get there a bit early. Laura likes us ready to take tables at our shift time, not just be walking in. She's a kind woman, but she runs a tight ship.

We walk to the back and up the metal staircase, Samuel's hand gently guiding mine up the spiral. We walk into his apartment and remove our shoes at the door.

"I'll be right back." He winks. "Make yourself at home." He disappears into his bedroom. I walk over to the wall of windows while I wait. I look down at the busy street full of vendors, shops, and people. There's a park just across the street where mothers push their children in strollers and couples stroll alongside each other.

I hear Samuel walk out from his bedroom and into the kitchen. I hear the cupboards open and close, but I can't pull myself from the incredible movie of 'life' before me. I look down at a ledge at the bottom of the window and see an ashtray full of half-smoked cigarettes.

Samuel comes up from behind me and places a small kiss on the back of my shoulder. I turn and see him holding two mugs with steam coming from them.

"I made some tea, English breakfast." He offers the cup to me and I grab it. I can smell that intoxicating mint on his breath, the same scent I couldn't get enough of during our night in the bookstore. I smile at the memory.

"What?" he asks with a playful smile.

"Nothing," I laugh. I lean in and bring his lips to mine, just briefly. I wrap my hands around the hot mug, warming my cold fingers. It's not cold outside, but it's not exactly warm either. I close my eyes and take a sip, allowing the hot liquid to fill my stomach and bring warmth to my entire body. I hear Samuel's rings clink against his mug as he takes a long sip, keeping his eyes on me. I smile as I run my fingers down the V-neck collar of his black T-shirt. I can tell he's had this one for a while. There's no print or lettering, but the black has faded quite a bit and I notice a couple small holes throughout the shirt. I poke my finger through one.

He laughs, "Yeah, I should probably toss it," he says and he scans his shirt, probably just now realizing how many holes there were.

I shake my head. "No, I like it." I smile.

131

"Well then, maybe I should give it to you," he says at a whisper, placing his hand at the small of my back, pulling me closer to him. I breath in his fresh cologne and minty breath as he takes my mouth in his. My one hand still holds the mug, but my other hand laces within his hair pulling his mouth deeper into mine. I hear the chime from the front door of the store, and we break our embrace. He groans.

"I should have left that bloody door locked!" He laughs. I glance at the clock and it's already quarter to twelve.

"Oh shit! I have to go." I laugh as I place the mug down on the coffee table and scramble to get my shoes on. I go to run down the spiral stairs before I pause; I turn back around and look at Samuel. He finishes lacing his second boot and stands, his eyes meeting mine.

"What?" he asks and runs his hand through his hair.

I plant a soft kiss on his lips and turn back as he follows me down the stairs.

Chapter Twenty

I wave goodbye to Samuel as he tends to the customer that walked in. I speed walk down the road and arrive at the diner with eight minutes to spare. I greet Lily as I walk past her and into the employee break room. I place my stuff in my locker, wrap my black apron around my waist and get to work.

The first half of the shift goes by fast. The lunch rush keeps me on my feet most of the time, but my tables were kind and patient. I approach one of my tables in the back with their food and place one plate in front of each person.

"I'll be right back to fill your waters," I smile and return to the kitchen. I grab the glass water carafe and begin walking back towards my table. I glance at the table right behind mine and my blood turns cold. My ears start to ring, and my heart rate elevates. My body goes numb as my adrenaline races through my body. I drop the glass carafe on the floor, shattering everywhere.

It's *him*. He's here.

I'm frozen with fear. My feet cannot move; I can't speak, and my vision blurs. My breath quickens as I try to pull myself from this statued state. He's looks straight at me, dark eyes piercing into mine. I want to run, but my feet have turned into cinderblocks, holding me in place.

"Payton!" I hear Lily yell as she waves her hand in front of my face. Finally, I'm able to pull myself from my trance and I see the entire diner staring at me, everyone is silent. I look down and see my co-worker, Todd, sweeping glass off the floor. I look back up at where he was, and I see the face of a different man with a horrified expression. I blink rapidly. He's gone. Well, not gone. He was never here. I was imagining him? The man I mistook for him did have a slight resemblance, but not enough to where I should have seen what I saw. My nightmares are following me into the day.

"I am so sorry," I plead as I try to help Todd grab glass pieces off the floor. I grab one and it slices my finger open and I begin to bleed.

"Oh my gosh, honey, let's take you to the back." Lily grabs a napkin from her apron and covers my cut, leading me to the break room.

"I am so sorry, I... I don't know what that was," I explain.

"Shh, don't worry about it," Lily reassures me as she run my finger under the sinks. Once the water goes from red to clear, she grabs a band-aid from the drawer. She dries my finger to reveal a cut about two centimeters wide. She places the band-aid over top.

"All that blood for just a little thing," she laughs. Laura walks in the door and runs up to me.

"Oh my gosh, dear!" She looks at my wrapped finger, "Are you okay?!" She's practically yelling.

"Um, yeah. I am now. I'm so sorry Laura. I don't know what came over me." I'm fighting tears. She waves her hands in front of her face.

"Oh, don't you think on it for a minute, all I care about is that you're okay," she says as she places a hand on my shoulder. "Listen, we're going to be fine here, okay? How about you take the rest of the evening off." She really is the nicest woman.

"Oh, that's okay, really, I didn't mean to cause a fuss," I explain.

"It is no fuss at all, you hear me?" She offers a warm smile. "Now go home and get some rest." She places a hand on my cheek and reassures me that the rest of the staff will be okay.

I gather my things from the locker and leave out of the back. I'm a little embarrassed by the scene I caused and would rather not face the crowd of people that were staring at me.

As soon as I leave, I can't help the tears that begin to fill my eyes. I cross my arms in front of me, trying to make myself as small as possible as I shuffle down the street towards my apartment, at least I thought that's where I planned on going. Before I know it, I'm pushing my way through the front door of the bookstore. I walk in and I see Samuel placing books on to the shelf.

"Payton?" he asks, surprised to see me. It takes a second for him to notice my tear-stained cheeks. He quickly places the book on the floor and pulls me into his arms. I begin to sob. He pulls me tighter, just holding me. He doesn't ask what happened, he doesn't try to offer solutions or advice. He does exactly what I need him to and just holds me.

After a few minutes my sobs calm, and I pull back and look at him.

"I saw him." I try to collect my thoughts.

"Saw who Payton?" he asks. "What happened?"

In this moment I realize that if I want any sort of future with Samuel, I have to tell him. I have to tell him everything. Why I'm here, who I'm hiding from, the nightmares… everything. I sigh.

"I'm ready," I say as I look into his dark eyes.

"Ready?" he asks, unsure of what I mean.

"To tell you. To tell you everything." I feel like if I don't tell him, I will burst into a thousand pieces.

He pauses, studying my face. He shakes his head and leaves our embrace. He walks over to the front door and flips the 'Open' sign to 'Closed' and locks us inside. He turns back around and clears his throat.

"Um, after you," he says as he gestures towards the back of the store.

Chapter Twenty-One

I walk to the back of the store and Samuel follows. I run my hand up the cold metal railing as I take each step up the staircase. We walk into the apartment and I remove my shoes. I walk over to the couch and sit with my knees pulled together. All of a sudden, I'm freezing with goosebumps all over. I pull my arms into my side in an attempt to warm myself.

Samuel disappears into his bedroom then reemerges with a large blanket. He walks up and drapes in over my shoulder. I pull it tighter around me and I see him glance at the already blood-soaked band-aid on my finger.

"Let me get you a hot tea." He smiles warmly and walks into the kitchen. After a few moments he returns and holds out the tea. I grab it and curl my fingers around the mug, heating my frozen fingers. He sits down next to me and waits, patiently. After a silence between us that feels like it lasts for days, I take a deep breath.

"I thought I saw him there. At work," I whisper, barely audible.

"Who did you think you saw, Payton?" he asks, helping me along.

I sigh. "My husband." I look up at Samuel and his eyes remain kind, without judgement, waiting for my explanation.

"He's why I'm here," I continue. "He has done things to me, awful things. Things that I've tried to forget but can't." I pause.

"The nightmares?" Samuel asks in a low tone, and I nod softly. He places his hand on my knee as I continue.

"I had to leave. And I did. But during our marriage, he had convinced me that everyone close to me was trying to sabotage our relationship, so by the time I had the strength to leave, I had no one to turn to. No friends, no family. I've left so many times, but every time I left him, he found me. Every. Single. Time." Samuel tightens his grip on my knee, coaxing me to continue.

"So, one day, I packed everything I could into my backpack and thought that the only way to escape him was to leave the country so that he couldn't follow me. New phone, new credit cards, new life. I've always wanted to visit England since I was a kid, so looked at a map, closed my eyes, and decided that I would buy a ticket to wherever my finger landed." I shrug. "So here I am." I place the mug on the table.

"But I haven't escaped him. He's still here. In every thought, in every nightmare. It seems like the farther I get from him physically, the deeper he burrows himself into my brain."

A small tear runs down my cheek. Samuel lifts his hand to my face and catches the tear before it rolls off my face.

I clear my throat.

"I used to be really happy. We were really happy." I pause. "But not any more... and not like I am with you. Being with you feels... different." I look up at Samuel. He smiles and brings his forehead to mine.

He puts his hand on my chin and tilts my lips to his. The kiss is soft, tender, and safe.

"I'm glad you told me," he whispers.

We sit together in silence for a while before I clear my throat.

"Can you... tell me about Allison?" I ask hoping it'll make me feel less vulnerable.

His eyes widen. He sits back and runs his hands through his hair.

"You don't have to." I can tell the topic makes him uncomfortable. "I'm sorry. I shouldn't have."

"No, it's okay. I just don't ever really talk about her," he replies.

"Why?" I ask.

He pauses, deep in thought. "I don't really know, I guess. She really was an incredible person. I *should* talk about her more." He smiles, and I smile back. He continues. "We started dating in high school. My friends knew I was really into her, so they dared me to ask her out, and I did. And we were pretty much inseparable ever since." He looks down and picks at the chipped black polish on his nails.

"Sarah loved her, and my dad loved her. My dad thought she was good for me. And she was. I just wish I could have been as good for her as she was for me." His eyes go dark and he clears his throat.

"I started hanging out with a pretty bad crowd, parties and different drugs every night. At first, she fought me on it, and we'd get into huge fights every time I came home high. Then, eventually she got wrapped right up into it with me. Maybe she wanted to experience what was so important that I was willing to give up my life for it. Give up her. She just didn't want to lose me. So she joined me." He turns and looks at me. "She was such an incredible person... before me." I place my hand on his.

"But you're different now," I remind him.

He looks down at the wooden floor.

"Yeah, too bad it took her death to get me here. It was my wake-up call, my rock bottom. Well, not until after months of so many drugs I couldn't even try to remember where I was or who I was with. Her family will never forgive me for how I influenced her, and I probably won't ever forgive myself. If she'd never met me, she'd still be here."

I place my forehead on his shoulder and wrap my fingers in his. There's so much I want to say. Like how it isn't his fault and how she was her own person and made her own choices. And how incredible he is now, and how despite the horrors we've both experienced, it brought us here... together. But I can't find the right words, so we sit together, in silence.

Chapter Twenty-Two

I wake up and realize I'm still at Samuel's. His arm is around me and his head is leaning against the couch. We must have dozed off. I've had a really long day, and clearly needed some sleep. As I sit up, he stirs underneath me but stays asleep. I stand and walk over to the windows and watch a group of kids race on their bikes.

"Are you okay?" I hear Samuel ask me in a raspy voice. I turn around and he has a groggy look on his face, but he's smiling.

"Um, yeah, I am." I smile back as he walks over to me.

"You sure?" he asks as he places his hand on my shoulder and squeezes gently.

"Well, I mean, I smell like diner food." I laugh as I look down at my greasy work clothes, "I think I should head home and take a shower." I look at the clock on the wall and it reads 7.05 p.m.

"Oh… okay." He shrugs and pushes his hands into his pockets. I get on my tiptoes and press his lips to mine. As I pull away, I see him smile.

I walk down the metal staircase and into the bookstore with Samuel following behind me. I get to the door and I turn to look back at him. He's grabbing the books of off the floor that he placed there earlier when I came barreling in, face wet with tears. I feel a heaviness in the room, between us. Samuel is looking down at the books he just picked up.

"I'll, uhm, see you later then?" I ask, feeling nervous. He nods and offers me a quick smile.

It's not that we need to spend every second of every day together, but we did just share some heavy stuff about our lives to each other. I don't know what I was expecting, but I guess it just wasn't this. Maybe revealing the mystery dissipated 'the magic'. I know I sound stupid.

I get to my apartment and drag myself up the stairs. I undress on the way up. I leave my clothes on the floor of my bedroom and walk straight into the bathroom. I have to get the diner smell off me. I love the smell of greasy delicious food, just not in my hair or on my clothes.

I turn on the shower, wait for the warm water to take over, and step in. The water is incredibly hot and much needed. I allow the water run over me, washing the day off. I close my eyes, and *his* face flashes across. I close them tighter, but the tighter I close them the clearer his face becomes. I open my eyes and let my head fall back, staring at the ceiling. I've been running for so long, yet he still catches up with me, one way or another. It exhausts me.

I finish up and step out of the shower before the water has a chance to run cold. I walk to the closet and grab my comfiest, and least flattering, pajamas I own. I walk over to my bag and rummage through to find lip balm, when I feel fabric balled up at the bottom. I pull it out and my chest feels warms. It's Samuel's black T-shirt. The one he put on this morning. I pull it to my face and smell his cologne mixed with the smell of him. I didn't even notice that he had changed his shirt. I guess it would be hard to notice since he mostly just wears black. He must have changed and slipped it into my bag while I was asleep. This brings me relief, since I felt a strange feeling between us when I left the bookstore. I pull off my button-up pajama shirt and pull Samuel's shirt over my head.

I walk downstairs and begin to make myself a cup of tea. A hot shower, hot tea, and some rest. It's all I need to find relief from the day. Well, that and Samuel, but he's clearly busy this evening, or doesn't want to see me tonight. When I mentioned that I had to leave, he didn't seem interested at all in coming back to my apartment with me. But we have been spending a lot of time together. Maybe he just needs space.

I grab my cup of tea from the kitchen and begin walking over to the couch when I hear a knock at my door. I freeze. I start to fight flashbacks of times he has found me. He would find out where I was living and come banging on my door, begging, or demanding, me to come with him. He finds me, every time. My heart rate increases with my breathing. I hear the knocking again. I can't move. What if I did see him today? He's found me... again. I don't even feel my hands drop the cup until it crashes on the ground, shooting shards of broken ceramic everywhere. My body feels numb, once again. I hate this effect, this chokehold, he has on me.

I don't regain feeling until I hear a voice from the other side of the door calling my name. It's Sam. When my body regains its ability to move, I walk over to the door and open it. I look out and see Samuel step on half of a cigarette with his boot.

He looks up.

"Hey, are you okay? I heard something break." He looks behind me at the shattered pieces on the ground.

"Oh, um, yeah. I just dropped... wait, what are you doing here?" I ask, trying not to sound too needy or excited. He runs his hand through his hair.

"I, uh... to be honest." He laughs at himself. "I just really wanted to be near you. I know we've been together a lot lately and I understand if you would rather have your space I just..." he trails off. "I just really enjoy your company and was hoping to join you." All I can do is smile and open the door wider, signaling for him to come inside. I turn to follow him in, and I look down. I am in my most juvenile pink fuzzy pajama pants, wearing his shirt, with my wet hair frizzing up with each passing minute.

I grab the hair tie on my wrist and pull my hair into a bun, smoothing the fly-aways into my hair. And here's Samuel, looking incredible, as usual. He puts in minimal effort yet always looks incredible. Of course he's wearing his leather jacket, the jacket I have grown to find so much security in.

144

"Earlier, things just felt a little… I don't know. Am I being stupid?"

He smiles.

"No, I'm sorry. I just haven't discussed Allison with anyone, and I know you haven't discussed your stuff with anyone. It was just a heavy afternoon. I'm sorry if you felt… I don't know. I'm sorry. I just needed a minute to clear my head." I smile and nod back.

He walks over and begins to pick up the broken pieces off the floor.

"Oh, Sam. I got that, please," I say as I grab a towel off the counter. I bend over and soak up the splattered tea covering the floor.

"Please, let me help," he smiles. He finishes picking up the pieces and takes them over to the garbage. He turns back and looks at me and scans my shirt.

"Nice shirt," he smiles as he looks down, almost bashful. He looks back up at me and I laugh and roll my eyes.

He walks over to me and places his hands on my hips, gripping down. He leans in and touches his lips to mine, and I smile into the kiss. I can feel the want between us. He walks into me, slowly, pushing me towards the kitchen counter until my back meets it. He parts my lips further and traces my tongue with his. I taste the mint on his tongue, mixed with the taste of cigarettes. I usually cannot stand the smell or taste of cigarettes, but on his tongue, I've never tasted anything sweeter. I feel the scruff on his face scratch against my skin.

He pulls back. "I'm sorry, that's honestly not why I came, I swear." He laughs as he runs his hands through his hair. "I just can't help myself around you." His eyes darken.

"Sam," I whisper, "it's okay." I pull his lips back to mine.

Samuel tightens his grip around me and lifts me onto the counter. My breath quickens. He parts my legs with his torso and presses himself closer to me. I wrap my legs around him and continue to pull him into me.

"Sam," I say as I gasp for breath, "I don't want space from you. Ever." I run my hand into his hair and gently grip tighter. I feel him smile in our kiss and push deeper into my mouth. I feel his hands move to the waistband of my pants. I lift my hips up off the counter, allowing him to move them down my legs and onto the floor. He takes his calloused hands and runs them gently up my thigh. He leans down and plants small kisses that follow his hands. He gets to my underwear and runs his fingers along the waist band. I go to remove my T-shirt, well Sam's T-shirt, and he stops me.

"Leave it on," he whispers. "I love seeing this on you." He runs his hands under the shirt and cups me. I gasp at the cold sensation left by his rings and lean my head against the cupboard. He begins planting small kisses down my neck. I moan his name and start to feel myself pulse on the counter. He takes my mouth back in his and moves his hands back to the waistband of my underwear. He runs his fingers along the top before moving towards the center. He slides the fabric to the side and gently inserts two fingers. I gasp and grip the counter. He takes his other hand and grabs both of my hands in his one and moves them above my head, pressing them against the cupboard, pinning me. He's gentle, but strong, making it to where I cannot move my hands. He begins to move his fingers back and forth while using his thumb to circle around my nerves. I squirm with his touch. He goes slow, too slow.

"Sam," I beg him for relief. He pauses his fingers, drops my hands and moves his hand to my chin.

"With time, baby," he whispers. He takes his hands and grips my hips, sliding me closer to the edge. He takes my underwear and slides them down my thighs and drops them onto the floor. He looks at me and smiles, his eyes darkening. He leans down and plants kisses on my thighs as he bends his knees, settling on the floor. He takes my legs and places them over his shoulders. He wraps his arms around my thighs to keep me still, and I grip one hand on the countertop and one in his hair. He brings his tongue to my center and circles around, offering a gentle tease. His scruff runs across me, adding friction, pushing me further. I can't help but buck my hips, bringing me closer to him. I hear him moan as he takes me completely in his mouth. He hums, offering a light vibration as he sucks and teases my nerves. I rock my hips back and forth involuntarily. I begin to build higher and higher, the pit in my stomach growing.

"You taste fucking incredible when you're turned on," he says breathlessly, continuing to take all of me. My head slams against the cupboard as I try to find my breath. He takes one hand off my thigh and pushes two fingers into me, sending me into oblivion. I come undone under his touch, gripping his hair harder as he continues his pace until I've finished completely. I feel like ten minutes have passed before I'm able to stop writhing.

My eyes stay closed as I try to bring my heart rate back down. I feel him stand up as he runs his hands around my waist, helping me off the counter. I'm barely able to stand.

"Not gonna lie," he whispers, "I'm pretty proud of that one." I look at him and smile while he runs his hands through his hair. I walk up to him and slide his leather jacket off his shoulders. He allows it to fall and tosses it on the counter. I take his hand and walk him over to the couch. Once we're in front of the couch, I undo his belt along with his black ripped jeans and slide them down, allowing him to step out of them. Then, his briefs follow. I take his shirt and lift it over his head, tossing it on the coffee table. I run my hands along his chest, feeling every muscle beneath his skin, focusing on the small patch of dark hair in the center. Goosebumps cover his skin. I give him a gentle push towards the couch, and he takes the hint and sits down. I place myself on to his lap, with my legs on each side of him.

I gently grip him and sit down on top, going slowly to feel every bit of him. He gasps. I begin to move up and down, his hands on my hips guiding me. I feel him growing with each pulse.

"Wait," he whispers, "I don't have a... I didn't bring a..." he tries to find his breath.

"It's okay," I lean down and lightly press my lips to his. "We're okay," I hint.

"Are you sure?" He looks up at me. I nod back, He wraps his arms around me, and I glide myself up and down.

"Thank God, because feeling you without a condom is the most incredible feeling," he moans. I run both of my hands up through his hair as I inhale the intoxicating scent of his cologne. His grip is still around me guiding himself. I bring my forehead to his and watch him as he groans underneath me.

"I could fuck you forever," he whispers. The pit in my stomach starts to grow again. His words seem to have that effect.

"Promise?" I ask, and our eyes meet. He pauses.

"I promise," he replies as he takes my mouth in his, continuing his movements, moaning my name as we peak together, wrapping each other into a tight embrace.

We both hold each other as we allow ourselves to come back down from our euphoric state.

"I mean it," he whispers, still out of breath, "I promise."

Chapter Twenty-Three

I never *really* thought about the longevity of Sam and me. I've only been here a couple months now and I've fallen for him. Hard. He says and does all the right things. And I'm sure the fact that he's the most incredible looking man I've ever seen helps. He feels safe and secure but also turns me on like no one has before. But I barely know him. Don't get me wrong, the parts I do know are incredible. But what happens if *he* finds me and I have to leave? Would Sam leave his sister and the bookstore to come with me? Or am I setting myself up for what could be one of the biggest heartbreaks of my life. But here we are, promising each other. But promising what? Forever? Or the concept of forever? Or are we just promising possibilities?

"Payton?" Sam pulls me from my thoughts. "Are you okay?" he asks, refastening his jeans.

"Um, yeah," I reply as I walk over to the kitchen and find my bottoms.

"Are you sure?" he asks. He sits down on the couch and puts his elbows on his knee, hunching over. He looks confused, like he's trying to read my thoughts. I nod, unconvincingly.

"Listen," he begins as he walks over to me. "I know we haven't known each other long, but there's something about you…" he pauses, "I feel like I've known you for much longer than I have." I study his face, waiting for him to continue.

"And I'm not quite sure what we've just promised each other, but I could only hope it's something meaningful." He finishes. Maybe he did read my thoughts. I take a breath in.

"I just come with a lot of complications," I whisper.

"We all do." He brings his hand to my cheek, caressing my face in his rough, but incredibly warm, touch.

"Did you not hear anything I said earlier?" I laugh, reminding him that my past, present, and future, is no picnic.

"Did you hear anything I said?" he laughs, reminding me of the same.

"You're amazing, Sam. You say and do all the right things," I reply.

"Oh yes, former junkie that gave his girlfriend the drugs that killed her. So amazing." His eyes grew dark. My heart aches for him.

"Don't put me on a pedestal Payton." He lowers his forehead to mine. "I have to fight every day to not be that person any more. But having you around lately has made the fight so much easier." He presses his lips to mine, giving me a kiss so filled with want and passion that it nearly takes my breath away.

"I'm falling for you, Payton," he whispers, "and no amount of skeletons in your closet are going to make me stop."

He looks up at me and studies my face. My legs feel weak and my chest warm. I look into the eyes of what feels like my savior, pulling me out of a dark place every time we're together. The future still so unknown but at this moment, I don't care. I run my hands into his hair and take his mouth in mine. I feel him crave me more and more with each kiss. He presses his hips into me, and I feel him, ready again.

We spend the next few hours, even though it felt like days, making love. Over and over again, in almost every room of the apartment. We are insatiable. Craving and wanting each other more each time. Studying each other's bodies to perfection.

In between we talked, learning more about each other. I learned that Sam's mother died when he was a child and his father stopped speaking to him after Allison died. His father was hoping her death would be Sam's wake up call to get clean, which it was, just not fast enough. At first, it just drove him deeper into his addictions, trying to numb himself of all feelings, and nothing was off limits. He felt he didn't deserve to feel good feelings, but was afraid of the bad ones, so he kept himself high. When his dad died, and Sam learned that his father had left him the bookstore. He thought it was his father's way of making sure he failed one more time. But after toying with the idea of selling it, and his sister begging him not to, he thought maybe, just maybe, this was actually his father's last attempt to help Sam get his life together. To give him something to care for and be responsible for.

"So, one day, I was just done," he continues. "And I haven't used or drank since." He rolls over in the bed and looks at me, his lips swollen from our hearty appetites. I bring my hand to his jaw and trace my fingers over the stubble. I study the darkness in his eyes, understanding, now, where it comes from. We both have darkness in our past that is always breathing over our shoulders, waiting for us to take a wrong step. I lean in and press my mouth into his, tracing my tongue over his, tasting him as well as myself. I have no idea what time it is, but my heavy eyelids are hinting that it is way passed my usual bedtime as I fight to keep them open.

Sam laughs softly.

"Go to sleep, baby," Sam whispers as he pulls me to his chest, wrapping his arm around me, creating my favorite spot in the world. He plants a small kiss on top of my head as a drift off to sleep.

Chapter Twenty-Four

I wake up the next morning to an empty bed. The divot in the mattress left by Samuel is still visible, and warm, so he couldn't have been gone for long. I sit up and look around, the sun is already shining through the window, illuminating the bedroom. I check my phone for the time and it reads eleven thirty a.m. I can't remember the last time I slept in this late. Granted, the evening was full of... exercise, and we were up super late.

I go to pull the duvet off me to find Samuel when I hear the stairs begin to creek. Samuel is making his way up the stairs with a mug in each hand. He sits beside me and hands me a beautifully hot coffee with the perfect amount of creamer. I prefer my coffee to look like a lightly toasted marshmallow, and Samuel once again is taking his black. He doesn't say anything to me, right away. He crawls into bed, careful not to spill any coffee, offers me a smile and leans against the headboard, inviting me into his chest. I move over, accepting his invitation and the coffee. The hot liquid warms my entire body as I melt deeper into Samuel. He plants a soft kiss on my head as he enjoys his own coffee.

In this moment, life is perfect. In this moment, nothing else seems to matter. Is this how it's supposed to feel? Being with someone? Loving someone? Not that I'm saying I love Samuel. But I could. Do I? I mean, I've only known him for a short while, but I may. It would be a no brainer. He's insanely handsome, kind, and understands both my mind and my body in ways no one ever has. He has demons, sure, but don't we all? He has a past addiction habit, and I have a husband that sees me as an addiction. We're both running from these demons hoping they don't catch up to us and drag us back down to the depths of wherever they may take us.

I shake off these thoughts as Samuel pulls me from them.

"Payton?" he asks.

I clear my throat after taking another sip of coffee, "Yeah?"

He laughs, "You just seemed like you were somewhere else for a moment, like another planet. Another world."

"Believe me, there's nowhere else I'd rather be than right here." I lean up and plant a soft kiss on his stubbly jawline. I kind of dig him with the five o' clock shadow.

"So, does that mean you don't want to do what I planned for us today?" He replies, teasingly.

I perk up, "Plans?"

He smiles, "I want to take you somewhere."

"Hm, like… to breakfast?" I reply as my stomach begins to growl.

His stomach returns a growl and we both laugh, "Well, yes. Breakfast first, but I want to take you somewhere. Some place special."

"Like?" I return.

"Like, my place."

I look at him strangely.

"Um, I believe I've been to your place. Got a lovely tour while I was there."

He laughs and studies my face.

"No, not my home. My place. I mean, I call it my place." He pauses. "You'll see, that is if you're willing to move today." He winks at me and plants a small kiss on my forehead. If I wasn't still so incredibly sore from last night, I'd take him again right here to polish off this perfect morning.

We both finish our coffee and make our way to the bathroom. I turn the shower on, and we undress as we wait for the water to turn warm. There's not much to remove since I'm still wearing Samuel's tattered black shirt and all he's wearing is briefs. I throw my hair up to avoid washing it since it's already almost noon.

As we're waiting, he takes a few steps towards me and brings his lips to mine. Initially, I was horrified. I have not brushed my teeth today and I can't imagine it's very sexy. I try to push this thought from my mind because Samuel doesn't seem to notice or mind as he holds me in the kiss for what feels like seconds and an eternity at the same time.

He breaks away from me and studies my face. "Payton... I... um," he stutters then pauses, taking a deep breath. "I'm just really glad to have met you."

I lean in and plant a kiss on his chest and pull him into the now warm shower. I take some soap and begin to wash his chest, shoulders, arms, and back. I'm slow, meticulous, taking in every tattoo, every muscle. Something about this feels so intimate, even more intimate than our evening of physical exploration. Once he's thoroughly clean, he takes the soap and returns the favor. Studying my skin, kissing me as he moves his hands. It feels incredible. I could stay here all day... that is... until the water once again goes from incredibly warm to freezing cold within seconds.

"Damn!" Samuel's yells and we both begin to laugh.

We jump out of the shower and quickly grab our towel and wrap them around our now freezing bodies. Samuel's winks as he walks out of the bathroom to get dressed. I quickly add some make up to my face and attempt to make my hair somewhat decent. When I walk out of the room, I am happy to see Samuel already dressed and waiting for me, because I am starving. I go to my closet and find a white T-shirt and my black jeans. I add my Converses once we get downstairs and we are out the door.

I'm not a huge 'large breakfast' kind of person, I'm more of a 'quick bite' kind of breakfast person, so we stop at the bakery just down the road and grab the usual, a blueberry scone and a blueberry muffin. Although, both are large enough to creep out of the 'quick bite' category.

"So…" I turn to Samuel as we walk out of the bakery. "Are we walking to this mysterious location?"

"Unless you're in the mood for a five-mile walk, we should probably drive." He laughs. I didn't even know Samuel had a car. Everything you would need around here is so walkable, so it's normal around here to not own a car.

We walk up to the bookstore and it looks like the bookstore has already been opened. The sign is turned to *'Open'* and all of the lights are on. We walk inside and I see Sarah behind to counter.

"Good morning, early birds," she jokes.

Samuel nods at his sister and turns back to me.

"Wait right here, I'm gonna go grab the keys." He winks and heads to the back of the store. Sarah stands behind the counter, trying not to stare.

"Um, I'm sorry if I've stolen him a lot lately," I offer.

"Oh, don't worry about it. He gets a little annoying after a while." She laughs.

"Well, I know he's kind of been leaving you here by yourself a lot." I feel bad that she seems to be the one to be picking up a lot of the slack with Samuel leaving the store so often now.

"Payton, please." She reaches to put her hand over mine that's resting on the counter.

"I haven't seen Samuel this happy in forever. He used to be here 24/7, literally. Sometimes I swear he'd go days without even stepping outside for fresh air. He needs the break." We both laugh, seeing as he actually lives here as well, and the thought of him spending days couped up here is totally realistic.

"Seriously though, he hasn't been himself like this since... well, just in a long time." She looks as if she's offered too much information.

"Since Allison? He told me what happened." Her eyes go wide.

"He told you about her?" She's surprised.

I nod.

"Wow, that's... he just doesn't talk about her, ever. He wouldn't even talk about it with me much. Only small bits here and there."

She looks towards the back and we see Samuel reemerge with keys in his hands and a fresh black shirt.

"Ready to go?" He looks at both of us and furrows his brow. "Um, did I miss something?"

"Yeah, I was just telling Payton how nice it is to see you act like a normal person lately." She laughs and looks over to me. I laugh too.

He rolls his eyes.

"All right then." He holds up his keys and adds, "Let's go." I follow him out of the back of the store.

We walk out to a car covered by a large tan sheet. He pulls the sheet off and my jaw drops.

"Wow, that's... wow." It's all I can muster. I know a lot about classic cars, my dad was a bit of an expert on them and taught me a lot growing up. And *this* is a beautiful cherry red classic car. It looks almost undriven.

"Thanks, it's a 1968—" he starts.

"Ford Mustang Cobra Jet." I finish his thought.

"Um, wow. Yeah, it is. You know classic cars?" His eyes widen.

"A little. My dad was really into them. He taught me a lot" I reply.

He laughs, "Seems like more than a little." I laugh back and shrug.

"My dad was into cars too; this was actually his. Didn't even start before he got his hands on it." He looks over at the car, admiring all the work his father must have put into it.

He comes over to the passenger side and opens the door for me. I climb in and admire the soft leather of the interior. He enters the car from the driver side and starts the engine. It sounds incredible and causes the entire car to vibrate, just a little. Samuel looks over at me, his ring covered fingers holding the steering wheel and his dark hair lying over his forehead. His eyes are dark, but with the way the sun is covering him, you can see they're actually a beautiful shade of brown. He smiles at me with his perfect teeth and I can smell the familiar smell of mint from here.

"Ready?" he asks.

I smile and nod, because in this moment I'd go anywhere with him.

Chapter Twenty-Five

The weather is gorgeous. It's sunny and warm and the wind from the open car window is blowing my hair all around me. I can tell summer is just around the corner, I can smell it in the air. I look over at Samuel and he has one hand on the steering wheel and one on my thigh. His hair is flying around his face in the sexiest way possible. I didn't think it was possible for him to be any more attractive, until right now. He looks completely in his element, so at ease. He glances over at me and offers me such a genuinely happy smile before looking back towards the road. He gently grips my thigh and I place my hand over his. I run my fingers over his silver rings and admire the tattoos that travel down his arm and onto his fingers.

The drive is only about ten minutes before we pull up to a dramatic, and overgrown, garden. Within the garden there are white pillars that travel down a walkway, leading to a large matching pergola. Beautiful vines crawl up the pillars making it look untouched in the hundreds of years that it looks like it has been here.

Samuel opens my car door and helps me out.

"Where are we?" I ask, looking at all the different shades of green that surround us.

"Just a garden. It was built in 1906, and now it's where I come to think." He smiles.

"*Just* a garden? This place is incredible." I continue to take in the scenery around me.

He laughs and takes my hand. He leads me through a long stretch of pillars before we arrive at the pergola. The pergola overlooks a large garden full of all types of flowers and plants. It's quiet here. It feels like we are the only two people within a hundred miles. I haven't seen Hampstead like this yet. I've only seen the busy city life that surrounds my apartment.

"It's beautiful." I have no other words. I glance at Samuel, and despite all of this beauty around us, his eyes are glued to me.

"Yes, you are." He smiles and I feel my face flush and I roll my eyes.

"So, this is your place," I say, matter-of-factly. I walk over to a railing and rest my arms against it, looking out over what looks like miles and miles of beauty. Samuel walks over and rests next to me.

"Yeah. Every time I need a breath, or a break, I come here."

"Does Sarah come here too?" I ask.

He shakes his head. "No actually. If she knows about it, it's not because I told her. I've never really told anyone about it; it's like my little secret spot."

"But you brought me here?" I ask, confused as to why he shared this with me if he's never shared 'his place' with anyone.

He laughs and drops his head, allowing his hair to hang loosely. He looks back up at me.

"Yeah, I did."

"Why?" I ask faster than I even thought it.

He ponders this question for a moment. "Well, I never really wanted to share it with someone else before."

He pauses for a moment. "And I know that you have demons chasing you too, and I'd do anything to help you escape them. And this place has helped me so much, so I'm hoping that it could help you."

He has so much sincerity in his eyes. I can tell he so badly wants to be my savior, my knight in shining armor. To whisk me away from this life and protect me in a new one.

"Thank you." It's all I can muster. We both look out at the garden allowing a few moments of silence to fall between us. After a while he clears his throat.

"Ya know, last time I came here was after I met you. After the first time I walked you home." He continues to look outwards.

"What?" I ask.

"I was so taken back by you. I didn't know what it was about you, but there was something. And I knew I wanted to get to know you, but I had reservations."

"What reservations?"

"I've been so loyal to Allison for so long, even after her death. I felt like I couldn't move on with someone else because I felt like I would be tainting what her and I had." His eyes start to gloss over. "And I still carry so much guilt and shame about what happened to her, that I felt like I didn't deserve to be happy with someone else because I'd just fuck up the next person too." He's staring off into the garden, but I can tell he's not actually looking at the garden. He's looking at Allison.

"And then I met you, and I couldn't help it. I felt such a pull to you. I came out here day after day asking myself what to do. Trying to find it in me to forgive myself enough and trust myself enough to allow myself to get to know you." He looks over at me. "I mean it Payton. When I say I will not let anything bad happen to you, I really mean it. It would fucking destroy me."

I can feel the intensity in his words. I can tell he means every single one.

"Sam," is all I can whisper as I place my hand over his. I feel so sad for him in this moment, but also so incredibly loved.

"I also meant it when I said I was falling for you. I know it seems ridiculous because we've known each other all of like…five seconds." He laughs at himself. "But I am. I feel like I've known you for so much longer. I… fuck… I…" he stutters and takes a deep breath, but no words follow.

I place my hand behind his head and put my forehead against his. I know what he wants to say. Do I want him to say it? Would it change anything? It's just words, right? How much power can they really hold?

Neither of us speak as our bodies stay connected; an intensity builds between us.

"Say it, Sam. It's okay," I whisper, without thinking. In this moment, I don't care about possible ramifications or *what-ifs*. Right now, all I want is to hear him say what he's struggling so badly to say.

He looks up at me and studies my face. He runs his thumb across my bottom lip, then my jaw, then down my neck. I shudder at his movement. His heart is beating so fast and so hard, I can actually hear it. I watch his jaw clench. He can't. He can't say it.

"It's okay." I place my hand on his chest. "I know. It's okay. You don't have to, I don't need you to."

I feel his tense muscle relax with my words. He brings his forehead back to mine.

"I'm sorry," he says breathlessly.

I shake my head. I understand. The last person he said that to was Allison, and he's terrified that loving someone new will minimize the love he had with her. And with that would bring more guilt, and I do not want to be the cause of his guilt, even if doesn't actually have anything to do with me. He's just not ready, and that's okay.

I bring my lips to his, taking in his taste and touch as deeply as I can. The smell of his cologne mixed with the mint on his breath has become so intoxicating it makes me dizzy.

"Let's take a walk," I offer when I finally pull myself away from him. He looks at me and smiles. He grabs my hand, and we begin to walk down the pathway.

We walk for what feels like miles until we arrive back at the car. He opens the door for me but stands in the way, facing the car and away from me.

"Sam?" I stand confused. I see him steady his breathing. He turns towards me.

"I love you, Payton. I do." He locks eyes with me, looking scared but relieved. "I am so in love with you and it scares the shit out of me. But makes me so happy at the same time." He smiles. I stand, staring.

"I know we haven't known each other long, but this last month has felt like an entire lifetime with you. And I just want to live in this feeling with you. I don't want it to ever go away. I lost it once before because of my own actions, but I promise I will never let anything happen to you. No matter what or who you're afraid of, I'll be here."

My mind going through so many thoughts. But my body ignores my mind as I pull him into me and lock his lips to mine. In this moment, the entire world falls away. There's nobody but us in the entire world right now. My breath has been taken from me, but life has also been breathed right back in. I'm home. He's feels like home.

He pulls me deeper into him, making us feel as one body. We hold each other for what feels like an eternity. So many thoughts are racing through my head, scared and happy ones. I pull back and look at him, his eyes glossy and face red. I smile.

"I love you…" is all I can muster. He said so many amazing things, but my mouth can't keep up with my mind. His face makes it clear that it's all he needed to hear.

His face lights up and his smile stretches across his face. He closes the passenger door and opens the door to the backseat. He pulls me in close and slowly moves me into the car. In this moment, I don't care about anything or anyone around us. He kisses me so tenderly I can barely feel his lips on mine. Yet the passion radiating from them is palpable. His lips slowly become more forceful with the familiar feeling of need. He needs me. I need him. While cramped and hot in the back of this tiny car, everything feels perfect. Our bodies connect and we make the most incredible love I've ever experienced. We then lie together in silence. But all we need is silence. Everything we need to say to each other is felt in the air.

I look up at him and he wipes my hair off my sweaty forehead and plants a soft kiss right in the center.

"I didn't even know I could be this happy." He smiles.

"I didn't know love could feel this happy," I reply.

Chapter Twenty-Six

The ride home from the park was quick, too quick. Watching him from the passenger seat, watching his dark hair fly around from the all the windows being open. The huge smile beaming across his face showing him in pure bliss. If there was a heaven, that was it.

By the time we get back, the sun has nearly set. He walks over to my side of the car and opens the door for me. I stand up and he takes me in his arms, hold me by the small of my back up against the car. He kisses me so deeply, like he's been waiting the entire ride home to touch me. I don't think I've ever felt so loved, so needed.

We walk into the bookstore and there are books thrown everywhere.

"What the fuck?" Sam whispers.

I look around, and not only are there book thrown off the shelves, but pages are ripped from the books and scattered around like confetti. Shelves are knocked over and the front door is shattered.

"Goddammit! I bet you it was those fucking kids from the other day!" Sam yells.

"Kids?" I asked softly.

"Yeah, I kicked a couple of kids out the other day because they were shoving books into their backpacks." Sam runs his hands through his hair in frustration.

I feel my cell phone start to vibrate, which is strange since not many people have my number.

"I'll let you get that," he says with a sigh and starts to pick up some of the books. I pull my phone out of my pocket. The caller log says 'Unknown'. Typically, I would just send them to voicemail, but something made me want to answer it. I walk to the back of the store.

"Hello?"

"Hello... Payton."

My heart drops and the room starts to spin. I could recognize that voice from anywhere. From my dreams, my nightmares, my past. I feel a lump form in my throat. I can't tell whether I'm about to throw up or scream. I try and swallow down as much of this feeling as I can.

"How did you get this number?" I ask as calmly as I can.

"From the diner babe." I can hear the condescending tone in his voice. Then it registered what he said. The *diner*?

"What do you mean the diner?" The panic is starting to come through in my voice.

"*Your* diner, Payton. Laura is a sweet woman, isn't she? Once she heard about your poor, sick mother, she gave me your number to make sure I could reach out to you."

Tears start falling from my eyes.

"Don't you know this already, Payton? You're my wife. And I will always find you. And believe me, I know all about that guy you've been running around with. Oh, by the way, did you like my redecorating?" He begins to laugh.

I can't speak any more. I hang up and throw my phone to the floor, shattering it into pieces. My chest tightens and I feel like I can't breathe.

"Payton? You okay?" I hear Sam yell from the front of the store. I have to leave. I have to leave now and get as far from here as I can. I leave out the back of the store and begin to run as fast as I can.

I run up to my apartment door and frantically look around. What if he can see me? What if he's inside? Where is he? The world around me becomes out of focus as my adrenaline fires through me.

I turn the key in the lock slowly and try to steady my breathing. I open the door and walk in. Everything looks normal and untouched. I close the door behind me and shake my head. The door was locked; there's no way he could get in.

I wipe my face with my hands and take a couple deep breaths. I've done this before; I can do this again. But there was never a Sam before. I was in such a panicked state after the phone call, I didn't process that leaving again would mean leaving him. But staying would guarantee being found, and would also include Sam getting hurt, I'm sure of it. I don't even want to imagine what he would do to Sam, a man who's only wrongdoing was loving me. Leaving will break his heart, but it may also save him.

I run up the stairs and grab my suitcase and backpack from underneath my bed. I begin to throw everything I own in both bags. It only takes me about ten minutes since I've learned to travel light. As usual, I leave behind all the big items like blankets, pillows, and towels. This isn't my first time.

I race down the stairs and swing open my door. As I run out, I run right into a man. I shut my eyes and begin to sob as I drop to the ground. He was waiting for me, and now he has me in his grasp.

"Payton? What's going on?!"

It's Sam. I look up and see the man I love so incredibly worried for me. I stand and wipe my face. Sam scans my luggage next to me.

"What's happening? Where are you going?" he asks softly.

It takes a moment for me to muster the words.

"I'm leaving," I whisper.

"You're leaving? What do you mean you're leaving? Where?" His face is starting to look pale.

"I mean I've been here for too long. I need to keep moving. And it's time for me to go," I say it a little louder than I mean to. My eyes start to water once again.

He takes a step back.

"What?" he says so softly I could barely hear him. "I just... I'm confused. I love you Payton, and I thought you loved me." His face goes from pale to red.

"Maybe this is just all too much," I lie. "And maybe I shouldn't have dragged you into all this mess."

"What mess? What is going on, Payton?" Tears start to fall down his cheeks.

"I'm so sorry, Sam. I can't love you, and I have to go." I push past him and begin to walk, almost run, towards the nearest bus stop. It takes everything in me to not turn around and tell him what is actually going on, but I can't. If I tell him that my ex-husband found me, he'd just want to be my savior, and get himself hurt in the process. But if he thinks this is something I want, he'll be heartbroken but at least he'll be safe.

I arrive at the bus stop and the bus pulls in front of me. I look around and make sure I don't see anyone who may be following me before stepping on. I walk to the back of the bus and look out the back window. As the bus pulls away, I see him. I see Sam. He's running towards the bus. He looks destroyed. He's screaming something but I can't make out what he's saying. I shut my eyes as tight as I can and begin to cry softly, trying not to make a scene and draw attention to myself. My chest feels like it's being ripped open. I open my eyes again and I see Sam kneeling on the ground, but by now he's just a small dot fading off into the distance.

I should have known better. I should have known better than to bring someone else into my mess. This is my life. The running, the hiding, the moving. I was wrong to get involved with anyone, especially someone like Sam.

Images of Sam's face flash in my mind mixed with images of my husband. I get a flashback of dancing with Sam at the bookstore, but then it's followed by images of glass being thrown in my direction. There's no escaping it. My tears run dry. Here we go, again.

Chapter Twenty-Seven

The bus pulls up to the train station. I gather my luggage and walk off the bus. I scan my surroundings, making sure I wasn't followed by either my husband or Sam.

I walk into the station and up to counter. I look at the board behind the soft-spoken woman behind the counter and look at the list of places.

"Can I help you ma'am?" she asks with a kind smile on her face.

"Um, I don't really know where to go," I reply. The woman looks at me with a confused look on her face.

"What do you mean?" she asks.

"I just need a ticket to somewhere far away, but small. And safe." I look at her and she furrows her brow. "Please, just anywhere." My eyes start to water. She looks at me sympathetically and nods her head. She prints out a ticket and hands it to me. I don't even look at the location, I just look at the departure time: eleven p.m. That's an hour from now.

I walk over to a small corner in a dark area of the train station and wait. I have so many thoughts trying to push through but I do my best to silence them. I breathe deeply, attempting to calm my nerves. I've done this so many times before and I can do it now. I keep telling myself that everything is going to be just fine.

"Now boarding!" rings over the speakers. I jolt out of the sleep I must have slipped into. I glance up at the clock on the wall; it's ten to eleven. Thank God for the announcement. I stand up, gather my luggage and tuck my ticket into my pocket. I start walking towards the platform when I see a familiar face walk into the train station. It's Sam.

I freeze in the middle of the station. There's no running, he'll see me. He scans the station before his eyes find mine. I begin to walk towards the platform quickly.

"Payton!" he yells. I walk faster.

"Payton!" he yells even louder before he catches up to me. He steps right in front of me, forcing me to a stop.

"Payton," he whispers. "Please don't go." He puts his hands on my arms, holding me in place, probably afraid I'll run.

"I have to," I whisper through my throat that feels like it is being forced closed.

"No, you don't. Listen, I don't know what's going on, but I don't believe anything that you said back there. I know you love me, and I love you." His voice cracks.

"You don't understand. He's found me." I begin to cry softly.

"What do you mean?" he asks.

"I mean he's found me." My voice raises. "He called me. He knows where I work. He's the one who destroyed the bookstore. He knows where you live. And he will hurt you. I told you this was going to happen. He always finds me. And I can't stay and let him do anything to you." I begin to sob. Sam pulls me into his chest. He holds me for a while until I catch my breath.

He pulls me back and hold me at arm's length.

"I'm not afraid of him, Payton. And I told you, there's no safer place in the world than with me. I promise." He speaks softly, like if he talks too loudly, I'll shatter.

"You don't know him. You don't know what he's capable of. And I've never been with someone else, so *I* don't even know what he's capable of when it comes to you. I don't know how far he'll go," I manage through tears.

"Nothing he could do could hurt as bad as this. As you not being in my life." He holds his gaze.

"Last call. Now boarding!" rings through the train station.

"Please Sam, I have go." I grab my bags and push past Sam towards the platform.

I get up to the open doors and turn around one last time. He's standing in the center of the room, watching me. He's a broken man. And it's all my fault.

I walk onto the train and allow the doors to close behind me. I find an empty seat in a cabin to myself. I sit down and my mind starts to race. I start to think about how the rest of my life will be. Running, scared, nightmares. How am I going to live the rest of my life like this? Am I never going to truly live ever again? Just twelve hours ago, I was the happiest I'd ever been. What if I fight?

Eventually I'm going to have to, and I can either do it by myself or with Sam by side. Then I feel this overwhelming clarity, this is it. I'm done living the life of a damsel in distress. This is my life. I need to take it back. I'm an idiot.

I feel the train start to move slowly and I jump up.

"Wait! Please! I need to get off!" I yell but nobody is in the cabin. I run to the door and try to push it open, but I can't.

"Please!" I yell as loudly as I can.

An attendant comes through the doors.

"Ma'am, what's wrong?!"

"I need to get off this train, right now," I say, almost begging.

"Ma'am, the train is already moving; I'm afraid I can't do that."

I look around and see an emergency stop pull on the wall. I run over to the box and pull as hard as I can, bringing the train to a forceful stop.

"What are you doing?! You can't do that!" the attendant yells.

"I'm so sorry; it's an emergency," I apologize as I gather my bags and jump off the train onto an unfamiliar platform. I look around, unsure of my surroundings. I scramble through the train station before finding a dark mop of hair sitting in a dark corner. He's facing away from me. I walk up to him slowly, trying not to startle him. I get right behind him; he has his head in his hands.

"Sam?" I whisper, embarrassed. He lifts his head and slowly stands up. He turns to look at me, unable to say anything.

"I'm so sorry, I just don't know what else to do. But you're right. Running away is all I've ever done. And I just can't bring myself to run away from you. I've never loved someone like I love you, and he's taken so much from me already. I can't bear to let him take you from me too." A tear drops down my face.

"Fuck," he replies, breathlessly. He pulls me into him and our lips connect. I feel his cheeks become wet.

"I promise I will keep you safe. I promise, Payton. We'll do this together," he says in between breaths.

"I love you, Sam," I say almost as a plea as I try to catch my own breath.

"I know. And I know you're scared. But I'm right here, and I'm not going anywhere." He rests his forehead on mine until our tears dry.

"Please, take me home," I beg. He plants a kiss on my forehead, grabs my luggage for me and walks me out.

Chapter Twenty-Eight

Sam parks the car right outside the apartment and grabs my bags from the truck. I'm in the passenger seat, terrified to move. Sam comes over to the passenger door and opens it up for me.

"Come on, baby. It's okay." He holds his hand out and help me out of the car.

We walk into the apartment and lock the door behind us. Sam brings my bags upstairs and I follow behind. He drops them by the bed and walks into the bathroom. He starts the shower and walks back over to me. He takes my hand and walks me into the bathroom with him. He undressed himself, and then begins to undress me. He tosses our clothes to the floor and brings me into the shower. He sits on the floor of the shower and I follow. He puts his back the wall, facing the shower head and sits me in between his legs with my back to him.

"Lay back, Payton. Let the warm water relax you." I lay my head back on his chest. He takes the soap I left behind and begins to massage my shoulders and my neck. He plants kisses around my hairline. This is a comfort and a human warmth I've never known to exist. Our breathing synchronizes and I swear our heartbeats do as well. I begin to cry. Not from sadness, but from pure relief of where I am and who I'm with.

"It's okay baby," Sam whispers as he wraps his arms around me and holds me.

"There's just nowhere else I'd rather be than right here," I sigh and we sit together and allow the water to shower over us for a moment. "But we should also get out before the cold water comes." I smile up at Sam.

"Ah, yes. You're right." He laughs.

We both stand and I turn the shower off. We step out of the shower and I find a couple of towels I left under the bathroom sink. I hand one to Sam and we dry off.

We walk back to the bedroom. Sam's towel is wrapped in a way wear it just barely hangs off his hips. His dark hair hangs over his forehead as water droplets collect at the tips before dripping down his face. His tattoos move over his muscles as he breathes. I find myself staring so intently and I cannot look away.

He notices my stare and walks over to me. He unwraps my towel and drops it to the floor. Then he drops his own towel. I take my hand and run it over his chest while the other grasps his arm. He stands still, arms at his side, allowing me to take in everything that he is. I want to memorize every tattoo, every muscle, and every curve. I look up at him and meet his eyes. They're kind, so kind. And so hopeful for us.

He moves his hands to the side of my face and holds my head in his hands. He leans down and our lips meet. I feel his wet hair dust across my forehead. I wrap my arms around his waist and pull him closer to me. He breaks the kiss and pulls me towards the bed. He lies back and pulls me on top of him. I place my knees on each side of him. He lays as I'm sitting over him. We have each other's hands together, entwining our fingers. I lean down and take his mouth in mine, so deeply. Like this is the last kiss I'll ever have. He rolls to the side and I follow, lying next to him. He separates my legs with his knee and connects us into one person. One soul. As he pulses, he brings his thumb to my center and massages gently, bringing a pit to my stomach. Both him and his hand pick up speed, bringing me closer and closer to euphoria. I take my hand and grasp his hair gently releasing a moan from him, which is enough to bring me over the edge, and he follows close behind.

"I'll never need another thing in this world, as long as I have you," he says in a whisper as he lays down next to me, facing me. I roll to face him and find my future in his eyes. I watch him slowly drift off, and I follow.

Chapter Twenty-Nine

He slumps over me, finally passing out from the liquor. I try to drag myself out from underneath him without waking him. His dead weight is so heavy on top of me, I can barely breath. I manage to get myself free and run out of the room. I run to the backdoor and bolt out of the house. I wince as I run on the gravel in my bare feet. I can hardly see where I'm going due to my tears obscuring my vision. I get to the end of the street and slump over, trying to catch my breath. I look around and there is no one in sight. The streets are so calm, it's eerie and uncomfortable. I stand back up, wiping the tears from my face. All of a sudden, I feel a heaviness behind me, an evil. My head turns slowly, like it's full of rust and must be forced to move. Finally, my eyes meet his. He smiles and clutches my throat.

"I'll always find you."

My eyes shoot open, the room still dark. My heart is racing, and my eyes scan the bed. He's still here, Sam is still here. I take a moment to bring my breathing back to normal. It's just a nightmare. Typically waking up from these nightmares gives me a feeling of panic, but having Sam next to me brings me back to a safe place. I study him as he sleeps, admiring everything about him. Even in his sleep he is still the darkest yet most beautiful man I've ever seen.

I get up from the bed and throw on Sam's shirt that lying on the floor. I need a glass of water after the night I've had. I smile as I reminisce the evening we had, but then I begin to think too hard and I become overwhelmed with sadness. Careful not to wake Sam, I walk down the stairs trying not to make the stairs creak too loud and make my way into the kitchen. It's so dark I can hardly see a thing, but I manage to make my way to the kitchen and fill a glass of water. I turn to take it upstairs when I see a dark figure stand from the couch. I drop the glass, sending shards everywhere. The air feels like it's been sucked out of the room.

"Payton," the dark figure growls as it takes a step towards me. I try to take a step back but run into the countertop. My heart is beating so fast I can hear booming in my ears.

"I finally found you." The dark figure stops. "I always find you."

He's here.

"I've been looking everywhere for you," he says, his voice cracking. My voice is gone.

He takes another step towards me.

"I'm so sorry baby, please, come home with me," he pleads. I grab the countertop behind me so hard I can feel my knuckles turn white. I want to scream so Sam can hear me. But I can't find my voice.

He takes another step and settles about three feet away.

"Please, forgive me. And come home."

"I can't," is all I can muster.

"Why?" he growls. "Because of him?" He flings his arm in the direction of the stairs. "You're *my* wife, not his." He takes another step, stepping on a piece of glass, crushing it under his boot. I can smell liquor on his breath. I close my eyes, tightly, and reopen them hoping this is just another nightmare. But here he is, still standing in front of me, growing impatient.

"Because of you," I whisper. He closes the gap between us and puts his dirty hand on my throat. He rips me from the countertop and throws me to the floor. I land my hand on a piece of glass, slicing my palm open. I close my hand into a fist and watch blood start to ooze between my fingers.

"Because of *me*?" he booms. "Everything you've ever had is because of me. I gave us a life!" He walks over to me, towering above me. He grabs me by the wrist of my now bloodied hand and yanks me up.

"I gave you a chance to come home with me on your own, now I'm not giving you a choice." I struggle in his grip but he's too strong. He tightens his grip, turning my fingers purple.

"She's not going anywhere with you."

I hear Sam's calm voice from the stairs. My husband's eyes grow darker than they already are as he drops my hand and turns to face Sam.

"She's *my* wife," he growls. "She'll go wherever I tell her to."

He steps towards Sam. I'm frozen, unsure of what to do or how this is going to end.

"I don't care what she is. She's not your property. And if she wanted to go, she'd go," Sam replies, balling his fists at his side.

My husband walks closer to Sam, their noses almost touching.

"Who the fuck are you to tell me what she wants?"

Sam looks him in the eyes and smiles, whispering,

"The man who's fucking your wife."

He takes Sam by the throat and pushes him against the brick wall at the end of the stairs. He uses his other hand and strikes Sam in the jaw. Sam's face is bloodied and already beginning to swell. Sam frees himself from the grip on his throat and charges into my husband, shoving him over the couch, and landing on the floor. Sam walks around and straddles him as he begins to strike him over and over again. Sam's fingers are adorned with silver rings that leave their impact with every strike. My husband goes from fighting back to completely limp after what seems like a dozen strikes. I run over to Sam and grab him by the shoulder, shouting at him to stop.

"Please Sam! Get off!" I scream as I finally pull him off. Sam stands and looks down at my husband, limp, gasping for breath on the floor. He turns to me and scans my body, noticing the blood covering me from my cut.

"Are you okay?" He brings his swollen bloody hands to my face. I nod. He pulls me into his chest and holds me still as I sob.

Our embrace only lasts a moment before I hear a click. I look up and Sam is frozen with a gun to his head.

"You should have killed me when you had the chance."

He smiles a dark smile: my husband's face so swollen I can barely see his eyes. Sam holds up his hands and doesn't move.

"I'll go," I whisper. "I'll go with you. Please. Just put the gun down," I beg. My husband looks at me.

"Why? So he can beat me to death as soon as I do?" he tries calling my bluff. But there is no bluff; I will go anywhere with anyone to keep Sam safe. I shake my head.

"He won't because I'm asking him not to. I want to leave with you."

I look at Sam to make it clear, I am being serious,

"Please. Don't." I whisper.

"If he does, I'll kill you both," he replies. I nod, knowing he's also being serious. I take my shaking hands and place it around the barrel of the gun, and slowly lower his arm.

"Let's go." I grab my husband by the arm and begin to walk towards to door. Once at the door, he looks down at me and smiles.

"No one will get between us," he whispers. I look at him, then he swiftly raises the gun back up at Sam. I hear a loud bang, and my vision goes black. My ears start to ring so unbearably loud that I collapse to the floor. My entire body is shaking. When my vision recovers, I look over at Sam, who is now lying on the floor, blood oozing across the floor. I can't breathe. No matter how fast or how hard I try, oxygen is not reaching my lungs. What have I done? What the fuck have I done? I go to run over to Sam when I feel *his* hand clamp down on my wrist, pulling me out of the apartment.

I try to resist as much as possible.

"Sam! Sam, please!" is all I can scream. I can't feel anything. This is the worst nightmare so far, except it's real. My husband is trying to pull me from the apartment, but I am trying to resist with everything I can.

"Leave me alone! Please!" I beg over and over again.

"Listen to me. You're either coming home with me alive, or you're staying here dead. You choose?!" he bellows. He drags me out of the apartment, and I see these lights from the distance. And they're getting closer, fast. It only takes me a moment before I realize it's police lights. One of my neighbors must have heard the gunshot and called. And I've never been more relieved.

The cops pull up fast and order us to put our hands up. My husband looks down at me with his dark, evil eyes and drops his gun, placing his hands on his head, and drops to his knees. I put my hands up as well and begin to cry. The cops rush us and put us both in handcuffs.

"Sam, he's inside. He's been shot. Please save him, please!" I beg in between gasps.

The cop says something in his transmitter and two other cops rush inside. An ambulance pulls up a moment after and EMTs rush inside. The cop takes me to the car to take a statement from me, and I see the EMTs bring Sam out of the apartment on the gurney. He's limp.

"Sam!" I scream and try to run to him, but the cop stops me.

"Listen ma'am, I get that this is all very overwhelming, but I need you to stay with me until we understand what happened here."

I cry as I watch the EMTs give Sam mouth to mouth as they load him into the ambulance.

I should have left earlier. What if Sam dies and it's all my fault? I should have stayed on that train and never looked back. These are my thoughts until I see my husband in handcuffs being placed in the back of a police car. Then I realize, it's over. Everything is over. The running. The stalking. The hiding. It's all done. But at what cost?

Chapter Thirty — Three Months Later

The sun beams into my window, breaking me from my sleep. I check my phone, it's ten a.m. I roll out of bed and sit on the edge in silence. It's been a few months now. Since everything happened. Since my entire life came to a screeching halt. I lived the worst nightmare of my life. Except I couldn't wake up from it. My entire adult life consisted of abuse and fear that turned into running and hiding. Hiding from a man who was supposed to love me. Then I found someone that was able to show me what love was actually supposed to feel like. The warmth, the kindness, that unconditionality. Sam embodied someone that I spent my whole life searching for. He's the true love of my life. I'll never love or be loved by someone like Sam again. It took only moments for me to fall for him, but it will take a lifetime for me to forget those moments.

I walk over to my closet and pick out my nicest black dress. Sam never saw this one. He'd love it.

I gather my hair into a low bun and slip on my black heels. I stare at myself in the mirror and think about how this apartment was my very own hell not too long ago.

I leave the apartment and walk towards the bookstore. I want to stop in the bakery a few doors down, Sam loved that place.

I walk up to the bakery counter and order a half-dozen of muffins.

"Make sure there's a blueberry or two in there please." I smile softly. The lady behind the counter nods back. I pull out my wallet to pay and she stops me.

"Oh hun, they're on the house today." She smiles and slides the bag towards me. Clearly Sam impacted more than just me.

I walk a few doors down and stand in front of the bookstore. The sign is flipped to *'Closed'*. I walk in and the chime on the new door announces my presence. I see Sarah in the back, and I set the bag of muffins on the glass countertop. I walk to the back and greet her.

"Oh Payton! It's so good to see you." She greets me with a hug. She's wearing a black knee-length dress. She's so beautiful, just like her brother. I help her set up some tables and chairs in the center of the store. I see friends and family start to file in, greeting one another.

The memory of our night together in the center of this store overwhelms me. I can still feel my face rest against his chest.

"Hey." Sarah pulls me from my thoughts. "You okay?" she asks. I nod.

As more people arrive, Sarah shuffles everyone to the center where all the tables are. She has Sam's favorite indie playlist playing through the speakers of the bookstore, the same playlist he played the night we spent here together. Dancing, laughing, falling for each other.

I introduce myself, one by one, to Sam's closest friends and family.

"This had to had been hard to arrange," one of his band mates says in passing.

"You have no idea." I offer a soft smile and stand, staring at the door. I see Noah and Olivia walk in and I wave them over.

"Payton! How are you?" Noah says as he brings me in for a tight hug and Olivia follows.

"You've been through so much. If you need anything, please let us know." Olivia says with full sincerity.

"Thank you," I reply as I squeeze her hand that's on my shoulder.

"All right guys! It's almost time," Sarah yells to the guests.

I stand staring at the front of the store. Sarah comes up behind me.

"You have to hide," she says as she smiles and walks away.

I hear the door chime and see a beautiful dark-haired man walk in my direction.

"Surprise!" Everyone yells. He jumps back.

"What?!" He looks at me with his beautiful smile. One I will always remember. He walks straight to me pulling me into a tight embrace.

"How did you do this!?" he asks.

I laugh and bring his lips to mine, then whisper "Happy Birthday, Sam. I love you."